ADAM AL-SIRGANY

MORE HELL

Stories, Tilled and Driftless

WHISKEY TIT
NYC & VT

Published in the United States and Canada by Whisk(e)y Tit: www.whiskeytit.com. If you wish to use or reproduce all or part of this book for any means, please let the author and publisher know. You're pretty much required to, legally.

ISBN 978-1-952600-62-3

Edited by K. Hank Jost
Cover design by Sébastien Derenoncourt

> L'enfer, c'est les autres.
> — Garcin

Now about fears and wishes. There's the fear of being intimidated by anonymous authority, and by the not-so-anonymous, into giving up ideas that might be risky and contrary, and there's the wish to never give in or give up. There's unease over the times my eyes deceived me or my wits deserted me, and counterfeit ideas slipped into the work, and there's the wish that it never happen again. There's remorse over the times my conscience looked the other way, allowing a story to attempt a trespass on someone's inviolable depths, and there's the wish to be forgiven. And there's the wish that the delusion I labor under will never lift off and leave me. What a delusion! Imagining that I, too, can divide the light from the darkness.
— Gina Berriault

> Eh bien, continuons
> — Garcin

Raise less corn and more hell—
                not Mary Elizabeth Lease,
but "a right good bit of advice"

CONTENTS

Boy Friends, Girl Friends, Former Lovers
    Allegro Non Molto   10
    Long Weekend   35
    Brokedown Palace   38
    Days Between   60

Lies, Damned Lies, and Statistics
    A Real Drag Princess   68
    A Probable Hypothesis   94
    Gracie's Story   97
    And Good Will Towards Men   102
    The Elves and the Cobbler   117

Heritage
    Driftless   121
    Law of Conservation   123
    Potluck   125
    Blackhawks   133
    ... a single charm is doubtful: a diptych   135
    Stars   147
    Samsara and Other Large Animals   149

BOY
FRIENDS,
GIRL
FRIENDS,
FORMER
LOVERS

ALLEGRO NON MOLTO

Jason stayed in Iowa City an extra night. Sober now, he stays out late. Fewer cigarettes. Harder dicked and nothing to come home with. Left his spirit in the bottle. Never was much, but was something. There aren't so many years between stupid youth and forty where a drunk's wet eyes aren't flattering, and Maria spent all twelve of them drinking with Neil Kenning to absolutely nothing at all.

It turned out to be one of those afternoons where there was nothing in the house but a half bottle of vermouth and white cooking wine. She'd kept less since Jason converted, had been to the store once already. The walk was beyond her now. Orange blossom honey, leftover from a Christmas gift, over little square cubes of ice, vermouth, a splash of water. Birth of ingenuity. Clavier à lumières. She put on Scriabin. Wondered what he needed that light organ for.

Maria undressed while the bathwater ran and got in and let it keep running. One foot to the wall, she pressed her body long, and wished, like always, for a tub she could sprawl in. She put her mug down on the rim of the bath and pushed the ice from one side to the other with the end of a finger. Old habit—slow, pacing. Everyone looks at you like you have them in mind, but it's the leaving room to choose. It's today what I'm trying to, and tomorrow what I want to remember. You have to keep three or four shampoos to bind the day to the way you wash it from you without the memory of scents.

She took a piece of ice between two fingers and lifted it, its cube gone oblong. The density of its cold fell away from her. She pinched it back into the mug, and again. A crotch of her fingers catching the edge. She tasted vermouth on her fingertips and again pinched, and came out with a cube she let fall into the water between her legs. It struck her thighs with a sharp, reaching cold. She swept it with three fingers so that it touched her softly with frozen bites on her lips, the skin of her legs, until it melted away and even the thin cool streams were gone. She drank her vermouth and listened to Horowitz at the piano, one of Scriabin's sonatas, stumbles and stomps, elegantly, and thought about the sweet way the old man's cheeks hung off their bones like an open curtain to his smile.

No way to remember dreams really. How full they are. When you write them down, the details fall away, just a riff, a melody.

Neil used to claim that was how you knew it was a dream, opening a book to scribbles. But she used to read in dreams and the shelves were full of small glass pieces without any bubbles at all. She just couldn't hold the memories long enough to rebuild the world. That could be the want. As if it were one. To see to where you're going. That mad Himalayan dance he never witnessed. *I am God. I am Nothing.* That meaningless vacillation.

§

Maria grew up in the North Chicago suburbs, in Highwood. Not on the lake, but in from it, on Prairie Avenue and Evolution.

What she remembers is the Seventies, mostly. Highwood was still middle-class Italian. So much so her father just called his restaurant Conti's.

The dagos would say, "Stephano, wouldn't it be nice if you had 'Italian Restaurant' up on the sign. Colors of the flag. You ashamed of who you are?"

He'd say, "My name is Conti. The first thing on the menu's panzanella. You want me to spend my time on your dinner or on telling some Jew where he's lost?"

He'd tell that joke, every chance he got, for the pat on the arm. The old Italians, she thinks, asked just to hear him tell it. They liked the wit. They liked the idea they so much owned a place their own that accommodation wasn't a question. That the gods of Chicago, of America, would have to assimilate to them.

The gods, of course, were not Jews, and not Jewish really. The Presidents always English, except the one they killed. The mayor Irish, then a Croat, then a woman—which was worse. Inflation was from the Holy Lands, about a fight with the Jews, sure, but caused by the towelheads. Her father's bank was Italian, though. He complained about the rest, complained the way he did, she thinks, to imagine there was loyalty somewhere. To believe someone was obliged to hear him in a world so full of demons.

His anger didn't help. Bankers, he'd explain, they're bureaucrats, they don't deal in your emotions. They don't understand human beings. Worse, they think like doctors. That you owe them. They don't really want to talk about your problems, but they'll blame you for causing them. They want to do their job. That's it. Even when they fuck it up, when they can't do anything at all, they want to be thanked for finishing the task of telling you to be hopeless. For calling the task finished. And there you are, broke. No home. No business. And an ache in your shoulder helped better by dry weather than aspirin.

When her father lost the restaurant, it was wintertime, the deep after-Christmas winter on the Lake. The few customers Conti's had then were wealthier, men who knew Stephano and imagined it would cheer him to serve a big meal with two bottles of vino.

And it did. But those men were realists, too. That's how they'd gotten to be wealthy. They knew that cheer is not salvation. That a business doesn't decline in a season. Vital as it might have been, it dies like men, by days.

By the end of January her father's friends, his favorite customers began asking where he would go next, began suggesting they'd like to see him again, maybe in Galena, where they weekended summers. They liked the getaway, the nature. Hated all that German crap and farmer food the local restaurants served. Land is cheap, they'd say. You should buy some.

At first, Stephano just repeated it back, that manic question, "Buy some?" He asked it, and he asked it, until the question erected itself into an exclamation, an affirmation, a cry. It echoed through the house, and the question took her mother, and the disease unfurled with that same grotesque progression, straight down the halls of the realtor's office.

The record ended. With nothing on the sound system but the needle's merry-go-round shoosh, her ear began to ring. She touched it, pad of her middle finger closing the hole. A certain undefinable pressure ached her on that right side, behind the lobe, down the jawline.

June, already summer, Maria poured more vermouth into a half-filled mug and put on a CD. One of those self-mixed relics of Neil. The now bled memories of road trips in a rusting Volkswagen Rabbit and a rustier Jeep Cherokee, where they slept with arms against the tire jack and a cooler at night. Neil always wanted enough Dead, enough Neil Young, enough Dylan—whoever it was they were traveling to see—to carry the spirit, not so much to drown it to nothing. A thrust into adventure, a drift to carry them home.

That was how he put it. This place, it wasn't where he'd grown up or even where he'd become a man, if that is what he'd become. It wasn't where he'd lived longest or best. Home to him was the stretch of towns and corn and roads from Northern Missouri to Southern Wisconsin, from Kansas to Peoria, a waving cross of the Midwest with Iowa at its center.

A year or so after their wedding, they'd left Iowa City. Tried to be urban for a couple of months, but the pace of anyplace interesting overcame them past the time of a vacation. It was who they were, who they'd become.

Still, Maria wished there were more in Galena. She lacked the storytelling perspective, a way to make meaning of it her own. So it was what it was, and what it was was a place you went if you were feeling daring and wanted to test your defenses against the prime export of a backwater village, airwaves that made the below-average appear normal. It was a place where occasionally you had encounters that made you wonder, 'Is this what life is about?' before the below-average again drown out aspirational thinking.

Earlier, at the store, a two-year-old boy trapped in a grocery cart in the checkout line had over-eyed a bouquet of flowers she was buying for her piano top. He leaned forward, his plump fingers on the cart, his soft chest pressing into it, his baby-fat stomach showing its remnants by his hunch. After walking away, she tore off a purple chrysanthemum, walked back. She was speckled with drizzle and so was the flower, petals soft-handing droplets. The boy turned around as she came through the double doors. He knew exactly why she was there. He took the flower without even a smile.

It made her happier than she'd been in forever, for a solid ten minutes. Was great. Like all those years of trying to drink the bar empty with Neil. The reverberating readiness of something nearly beautiful. Lifelike, sitting in a field in the rain, throwing matches at a firework.

Neil Kenning was the kind of boy who'd spent his whole long childhood learning tricks of that kind. At first, you didn't believe it. Then he'd do it again, and you'd adore him for his magic. Then you'd see how he'd done it, and be unimpressed until you realized you couldn't gather the magic yourself, that you lacked the dexterity. He might show you how to smooth your motion, but only if he had something new going.

And it would all start again. It was like watching other people play Hindemith—fascinating and aggravating. It was addictive, and by the time you knew that, you'd given too much of your life to it to imagine doing anything else. The town, a match, a match, black keys, a restaurant, a child.

She was lying on the couch when Neil rang the doorbell. She was half staring at the flowers on the piano, half looking at the sun droop over the balcony. He never knocked unless he was fooling around, so he never knocked on her door now that it was her door and not theirs. Maria eyed the clock on the stereo in the passing hope he was late, that that small injustice might save her from his dignified suffering.

That he was on time was no real surprise. He'd become punctual as soon as their divorce was finalized. As if the singular fact that she had caused and wanted the divorce were not enough, he came on time to prove the divorce itself, as much as Liv, was unalterably theirs. His timeliness a constant reminder he was obliged to return their daughter by the clock, and so for years yet Maria would be obliged to open the door to him and watch him staring her straight in the throat.

⚜

Maria started high school in the fall of 1980, full of anxiety as anyone. Only she, an Italian girl from an Italian suburb of a city full of Blacks and Irish and

Polish and Italians, she at fourteen already chesty but without her period or the hair her Highwood friends had told her to worry over trimming, she found herself in a town of a couple thousand, where it was not where her grandparents had been born that mattered—Sicily or Milano or Rome.

What mattered was that she was new to them, and worse, that she was urban, that her ass shook when she ran in gym glass. No one would speak with her. They said the same meaningless hellos they said to everyone, to the walls, the way checkout clerks ask if you would like your receipt. They waved with absent smiles when she said hi back, but they kept their distance, shoulders turned. And all of them leered, the boys especially, with a sense of anger and hunger that should have frightened her but became the only way she was certain she was there at all.

Then the older boys started to talk. In the halls between classes they'd say, "So you're new?"

She'd say, "Yeah."

They'd say, "From Chicago?"

She'd say, "Kinda."

They'd say, "Tig ol' bitties?"

She'd say, "What?"

They'd say, "How'd you like to ride out to the lake?"

She never took them up. Her mother would have raised too much hell. But never giving an answer didn't stop them asking. Every day one of them came, touching the door of her locker or following her through the parking lot in front of the school, which made for someone she spoke to every day. For a while the only, several someones.

Donna turned up in September, or October, maybe. Military daughter. Her mother was from Galena, she'd lived a couple years here while her father was in Vietnam. The Army sent him to a stable base outside Tokyo after a tour, so Donna's first memories were from Japan.

That she was pretty wasn't obvious, but she wanted it to be. She had long black hair that her mother poorly braided. When her father retired, she'd come to Illinois through Honolulu so had a tan unnatural as a sailor's, even everywhere and rough hued as stained leather. Some of the boys took her for foreign, so into that winter she did her homework by a south-facing window, in a bra and panties, trying to get herself some sun.

Maria learned this, she wasn't told, how Donna grew pretty undressed in daylight. They spent their afternoons together, in Donna's empty house, the two new girls who never made friends. Maria, the ice queen, and her skinny pal who smelled of cigarettes and who the boys took turns with in their fathers' trucks. They called her Hiawatha, even into winter when she cropped her hair like Blondie and managed a burned-out, at-home bleach.

Donna didn't care about her reputation, or about getting grounded. She was grounded, she claimed, until thirty-one, if her mother was really counting. She didn't care about her mother's disappointment or whether her father hit her. She had seen the world—on Army bases, to be sure—but she had been there and lived there. She had crossed the borders and knew, better than Maria ever would, there was nothing in the world to find better than being alive any place on it. It was a Beat ease Maria would never find in herself.

She was a virgin throughout high school. When Donna went out with boys around the lake, she would ask Maria to come. She would remind Maria how cute a certain boy was who might just ride along if she came too. "Come on, lover," she'd beg.

And Maria came, three, four times in as many years. She sat in the back seat with nervous boys and sipped MD 20/20 and tried to get them to talk while Donna's clothes came off. She would kiss them. They'd be hard already from watching their friend in hers, limbs fumbling over the front seats or backs rolling in the grass. Hard those watching boys would kiss Maria. She would let them under her shirt to touch the side of a breast outside her bra. She would build up tears, she would work up a scream. By then their friend had always finished and all she would have to say was, "Not now."

The girls would get dropped off at Donna's house and Donna would walk her home, up the hill, to the apartment Maria's father was building along the dining room of Conti's Italian Restaurant.

Her father liked Donna. He catered to vacationers, never took locals seriously. The farmers, the teachers, the odd mechanic and grocery store clerk—they preferred boxed pasta because their taste buds were trained toward economy. They'd order spaghetti and meatballs and argue—politely to be sure, but argue nonetheless—with him that it should be the same cost as the spaghetti because it was "spaghetti and meatballs," because that's what they'd expected. When the bill came they were always stiffly trying to pretend at indifference, but for all their anxiety about money they couldn't estimate tax and so always took offense at the increase, which they settled themselves to by whispering angrily at their wives and denying his waiters their tips. These people lacked class. Worse, they lacked culture.

Stephano admired military men, though. He felt as though an Army officer's daughter would be a good influence, finally give his Maria ambition. As if he knew Donna at all. As if attitudes caught like the flu. Which they do, which they don't.

He would serve Donna massive plates of ziti in the family kitchen, smaller corner pieces to Maria, nearly cheeseless and heavily sauced. "Donna," he would say, "you're wasting away. You have to eat. How can you focus in your classes if you don't eat, a twig like you."

"I do alright," Donna would say—which was somehow true. She wasn't brilliant. She wasn't stupid. She was smart enough to be smart without trying. Those evenings in the kitchen, she would tease Maria's father. "Don't you like skinny girls," she'd say.

"Any man my age," he'd say, "learns to appreciate a woman."

And once Donna got up, went to the door to the restaurant, unlocked it and looked inside. It was winter. There was nothing but three or four men drinking whiskey at the bar, tapping their glasses for Maria's mother to refill. "You think they appreciate women?" she asked.

"They're drunks," her father had said. "They don't appreciate much." He *maître d'*ed Donna back to her chair, and petted Maria's hair, and imagined, Maria supposed, the perfect shelter he'd made for them. But he'd told them both what they'd believe, despite themselves, that men were different from boys. That they would become something new when someone saw them differently.

While Liv got in the shower, Maria checked her pockets and backpack, threw the clothes in the hamper, listened to Neil pace the balcony, insisting on a chat. Maria gives Liv ten dollars just before Neil picks her up. Every time. In case he doesn't feed you, at least you'll have something to buy a sandwich with. She knows this is a threat, but an unimpeachable one.

She looks for signs of damage in the girl's long jaw. Every time. It's always fine. Small scratches on her knees, catching everything by a fall. Neil lives in the old house, on the slung-hilled country roads between Galena and Scales Mound. Half a mile from the nearest real neighbor, maybe seven miles to anywhere you could buy food from.

She wonders—she never sees the money again—if Neil collects it, his small, quiet alimony. Or if it just falls from a pocket and lives somewhere in the grass out there in the country while her daughter runs around, collapsing on her knees for the delight of it, never worrying about stains or tears, cartilage or ACLs or the future.

Never again will you be 14. Never again 20. Never 34, wise and young yet. Never 40. Donna was all her ages, but Maria was always looking back to the ages she never was, wishing she'd been them. To date, her body,

42, felt it, and Maria remained a cipher—even to herself. But Donna—

Donna—there's an age you get to when everyone you know is getting married, which is the reason you think you should, that the ceremony itself is the only thing keeping you from the life you said you'd never have.

Then there's the age you get to most of those people, most of your friends and acquaintances, are divorced or miserable. Old love affairs come hopelessly back by any means they're able. Old questions about yourself and what you are and what you ought to be and what you really desire. From old lovers, from yourself. It's almost flattering to think you're not too old for hope.

Maria spent too long in college, grad school. Piano performance at the University of Iowa, Iowa City, on the Iowa River. A place so far from anywhere there was only the one name. Someone told her once it meant the Drowsy Ones. Iowa. It was a place for young city kids to escape to and dream a few years before heading back, blankslated, to Chicago or St. Louis, to pursue careers they'd been sleepily practicing for.

But for Maria, for Neil, even for Jason, who'd tried harder to get out, Iowa was the city. The place their adolescence had turned to activity. Where Maria had taken two or three dozen men through her bed, certain they couldn't care for her, that in the way of her high school friend, there were many indifferent lovers. And it wasn't until many years later, when they started to find her online, to call and text out of the blue, she realized the indifference she'd affected to match pitch, she'd invented all of it. So had many of them.

Those sad boys who'd grown into sadder men, her indifference and her body were all they remembered. Maria, with her hair tied back, finding the power not to be free, but, to the man beneath her at least, to seem controlled, maybe even as though she didn't need his body. The cheap cotton sheets alive, rough gripping knees. Every small violence justifying adrenaline, the necessity of action.

Donna—these kinds of things never troubled her. She married a drunk, an older mechanic named Tom. They went to the same bars together. Drunk herself, she picked up men on occasion and on rarer occasion, some woman pitied Tom's collapse into a pint glass and took him home herself. Donna sold real estate, at the lake mostly. She had no need for college. In the middle-Eighties, the middle-Nineties, second homes were an easy sell. She lingered at the nineteenth hole of the golf course all summer, flirting with vacationing businessmen and dragging them through the staged beds of empty houses.

By the time Maria was home again, in earnest, Donna was comfortable, not only in herself but in everything, and it never looked so good as at exactly that moment, Maria realized, when a marriage and two failed moves later, she was nothing but an after-school piano teacher in a town where it couldn't have mattered less.

A piano teacher, without even the education to work at a school, like the talentless but credentialed twenty-something band director Donna, at that age, bragged about having had in the back of her car. In her thirties, her adventures fewer and more tame, she managed still to have the attitude she needed, the ability to be grateful for being seen beyond her years.

And the years kept going, which was the worst of it. They drifted from their thirties to their forties. Stephano died—cigarette heart attack at sixty-two—and left Maria the restaurant. She didn't know how to run it but had to, because her mother couldn't run it either. Maria had really thought that—had to. Because she needed an excuse to say there was no way out. No longer a pianist or even a piano teacher. A restauranteur, inherited title. Tragedy of life to *had to*.

She had to run the restaurant. Had to have a child, while she could. Because it had to be hers, theirs. Had to change her life to be who the child needed. Whatever that meant. Early to bed, early to rise, in imitation of a mother who'd failed her by being what she was supposed to be and a father whose business demanded it. Then it was her business, and she was nothing but its hopeless manager.

Maria went where Neil went. Had to, every trip, every backyard party chasing long-gone glory days she was never really a part of. Kissed Jason, because he'd kissed her at one of those parties, in the basement of his house. Had to. Had to let it happen, hot tingle of vodka and jalapeño poppers on her lips, on her lips. That manufactured, that bought, his tongue on her. With Neil and Liv upstairs and the rest of them who she'd only known through Neil. Had to leave because of what she'd done. Had to. What else?

Of course, you feel guilty, even for legitimate needs, but before a certain age there's time enough left you have to feel other feelings. Of course. Of course, if you were too old for anything else, there'd be no point in living in guilt. Anytime she was upset, Neil, always quoting that Kerouac line at her, "Anyway, I wrote the book because we're all going to die...."

What else. She turned the music down, put Scriabin back on, not because Phish was loud but because the change justified the time he'd spent out on the balcony, waiting.

There's a point at which you've been failing your own ideals so long and so completely that, even if you could come to yourself, you would find, reaching back, how much you'd aged, how little akin you were with former friends and former lovers, who too, many of them, had also failed marriages and become less than they'd hoped, but who'd done so with a fugal grace that gave their changes delusions they could hold on to. A faith in maturation that, to their minds, at least publicly, appeared like something other than a movement towards death. Having gone from C to G simply because it was sharper and next in the circle of fifths.

It all lacked sophistication, but hers, the not changing, was unintentionally flaunted, like one of those grad students who dresses down the banality of all compositions for his masterpiece not yet composed and who spends most of his days hanging paper clips and Mardi Gras beads from piano strings and getting the light right for his performances. She was someone who still, in her forties, resented boys like that, who wondered if they were all high school band directors daydreaming of their girl students and spending their evenings in the backseats of cars like Donna's. Someone who worried at *together ifs*.

It came to seem as though the acceptance of sorrow was life's meaning. As though to know this was not a realization but a surrender to truth. For all that you could come to know about disappointment and pain, for all the lost glittering newness of hearing Elgar for the first time, to know that that newness and homeostasis had in them no more meaning than the numbed and still aching now meant nothing more than the sorry recognition that, together, they were the only things that felt as though they did.

After Neil left her apartment, she went into Liv's room to see how their daughter was doing. Her mind rattled with that old sense of possibilities, future and past, with vague senses of ambivalence and shame, and the disappointment that even doing wrong lacks the joys and the woes of its promise.

Liv had gone to bed. Her bright blue towel lay half on the pillow, half on the sheet and the little damp nest of leftover wet stamped the pillowcase where the towel hadn't kept back her hair. She was awake, had maybe only tried to sleep or was woken by almost-familiar noises. "Hello," she said, and waved, smiling with exaggerated teeth.

"Hi," Maria said. "You're not asleep."

"Daddy says I sleep better when I run around."

"You didn't run around today?" Maria said.

"I went swimming today," said Liv.

"Well, that's running around in the water, isn't it? Was it fun?"

"Yes." She looked doubtful for a moment, then thrust her eyes towards Maria. "Can we run around in the water?"

"Now?" she said. "Not now."

"We left early," Liv said. "It rained. Daddy says you can't swim in the rain, because of lightning."

"Not now," Maria said.

"When?" she asked, leaping to the end.

Maria sat at the edge of the bed, watched the streetlights glow over her daughter's nightstand. She forgot the question. Forgot the body she was in, with its histories. Forgot the ache in her ear and jaw and temple, and noticing the forgetting by its sudden happiness, she felt tense again, shifted and stretched to relieve it, knew it there. "I don't know," said Maria.

"Why not," Liv said. "Are we busy now?"

"You have to sleep now," said Maria. From somewhere a little cloud of glow came rattling, Horowitz and the television, both of them on.

Donna had come into the restaurant last week, in the morning. Not with Tom or anyone else. She sat down at the bar and ordered a gimlet so she could ask Christopher, the bartender, if anybody ever drank those anymore and pretend to be impressed when he said, no, but he knew how to make one.

A man in a nylon navy polo sidled up to her while he did. He was their age maybe, bulky and confident, too confident for a forty-something drinking alone on a Tuesday.

He had a daughter, Maria knew. The way he eased close and eased closer, touching Donna's wrist, then straightened and raised a hand to frighten her for rejecting him. Maria hadn't heard what she'd said, but it had happened too fast to have been much. Donna turned back to the bar, indifferent as Dylan looking over a crowd. The man slunk into himself as quickly as he'd raised up, and retreated to a booth. It wasn't just Donna, she was sure. Someone had checked him before. He cared that she had.

"What are you gonna do," Donna said when Maria came out from the kitchen.

"I know," Maria said. "I just worry he'd do it." She bent across the bar and petted her friend on the back of a shoulder.

"You don't know anything about it," Donna at full volume.

Then with sudden calm, "Anyway, Chris wouldn't let anybody hurt me, would you, Chris?"

"No," said Christopher, and brought Donna her gimlet. She was almost as skinny as she had been as a teenager, all over almost indistinguishable from that younger self. The small differences in her clothes, the loose ruffled shoulders of her blouses, her pixie cut, the small apple breasts that had been pulled from her chest, the fine lines that comb-striped under her eyes when she put on a smile.

"Let's have a drink," she said. "All of us. Gimlets for everybody."

She waited for laughter she finally provided. Christopher excused himself, claimed he needed another coffee before the day, but Maria found herself on the other side of the bar taking an early wet lunch on a Tuesday. Jason was in Iowa City, teaching, playing backup sax for some pass-through band gigging Gabe's. Liv was with Neil. The restaurant could use, but never needed her.

They left Conti's after the first. Maria asked Christopher to let her mother know she was on an errand and would be back soon. She and Donna stopped off at the liquor store for a bottle of Bombay and stumbled up to Maria's apartment like two girls who were actually drunk, showing it to one another.

Donna fell back onto Maria's couch with the bottle and pulled her feet up, laughing. Her M.O. to be the center of things, and served. Maria didn't resist. Never had. Had hardly ever wanted to. She sliced limes and gathered glasses and ice, searched for soda water in the pantry. There wasn't any. She started to apologize, but Donna ignored her, filling their tumblers to the brim.

There's no place to play the etudes. They crash through any room like a lover waiting to break a glass against a wall, or you.

She put them on anyway, for Donna. For herself. She knew, after five minutes, Donna would make her one move off the davenport and put on an album her own. It didn't matter where they started. Scriabin was an easy no.

"It's too dense for my head," Donna said. "You have to learn to relax." The Horowitz came off so fast Maria thought Donna had broken the needle arm. "Something we can dance to, lover." Donna on her knees, filing through a crate of records in bunches of five or six.

"You can't even read them that way," Maria said.

"I know what I'm looking for."

Maria had asked if they'd had a nice time.
Neil had said, "Yes."
Neil had asked if Jason was well.
Maria had said, "Yes."

Neil had asked if it was nice to have a few days to herself.

Maria had said, "Yes."

Maria had asked when his vacation was again, if he had had any time to get ready.

Neil had asked if she ever missed him.

Maria had said, "Neil."

Neil had kissed her.

Maria had taken him by the back of his scalp. Held his hair, thick as it ever was. She'd said, "Neil."

Neil had turned her to the wall.

She'd pulled him by that hair back into the apartment and towards the door. "It's time to go," Maria had said.

"Mar," Neil had said.

Can you really have missed me so much you don't see that I still love you. In what way would it have stopped. Another lover.

It's that you go on and on and it's only with this one change, without satisfaction. It's that I get wet prodding liver scars. It's organic. It's meaningless.

Maria hadn't said anything.

Through the door he'd said, "Goodnight."

Donna had found the album she was looking for as much by color, Maria guessed, as anything. One of the Buddy Holly Stories. That yellowing eggshell, Buddy's face like a candidate for president. Donna took the record out and turned it several times on the balls of her fingers, surveyed the label before putting it on.

"Well lover, she asked, are you going to dance with me?"

They danced, in pacing circles around the baby grand that filled most of the living room. They danced, through part of "Crying, Waiting, Hoping," through "True Love Ways." Maria with her cheek on her friend's sharp hair and wishing she could be there without those thoughts, of sharpness, of the smells of Suave and cheap gel. Of those useless shames that reduce you like your parents do to being a child, those unrealized half thoughts of young love.

Three days later, it mattered less what had happened than that she couldn't ask what it had meant. Felt as though it must be something. Spent the whole week nipping at gin and haunting the restaurant, wondering what. Childish wondering, if it did or didn't matter. Wondering if it had as some brief but unnamed reification that now meant nothing because she'd waited to ask from it the good or the happiness or the escape that still cropped up vaguely at the edge of her mind, the way Beethoven saw great men, the way Mahler saw Alma, the way Scriabin believed in his Mysterium.

And most like Scriabin. Because she expected to die like he had, with the hazy dreamed effigies of the mind that die with you. Never having made the audience act, let alone witnessed the nobler beings you'd invented, half out of your own sadness, half out of other people's fictions. Anyway, she had never even seen one, a nobler being. Or if she had had there would be no way to know.

There would be no encomiums. No symphonies. No students praising what she'd given them. There would be slim memories of middle finger over left hand, thumb under right. There would be the restaurant, her father's sublimation of the same and better elsewhere, this Conti's that catered to weekenders and scrimping teenage romances and the unbearable semblance of a middle class that worked desk jobs in a land of farmers. And there would be Liv, who, if she got anything from her mother, would get a body Maria didn't want and Stephano's ability to see what shit everyone was full of, most of all herself.

Seeing it never stopped the sprawl. Three days later, Maria wondered what Donna knew and worried, despite herself, Donna knew something she didn't. That what Donna knew mattered most, because she had felt something for Donna and Donna—

It was possible for Donna to have a passing mood. To enjoy or not enjoy and to know and not need tomorrow.

The vermouth was gone. She'd put away the honey. Washed the dishes. Neil was gone. She'd thought it all out so many times the memories were blending. She'd eaten toast. Been to bed and the toilet, each several times. Got up to fill the piano's humidifier. It didn't need filling. The water set her off, though, and she sat a while on the toilet.

The Sun was still hours behind the Earth. Maria gathered the towel Liv was sleeping on around her daughter. She placed an arm behind her shoulders. "What do you say we go run around the pool?" she asked.

Liv gripped her mother's ribs and mumbled an inaudible question.

"We're going to the pool, love." She took Liv by the arm and pushed her towards the bathroom. Maria could almost see it, outside herself, the too fast way she yanked her daughter's nightshirt over her head, the hurried pulling of her limbs through a swimsuit. She could almost see Liv, scraping feet through the kitchen and over each stair, in the bob between anxious excitement and sleep that kept her head lolling against the window of the Cavalier while they drove into the Territories, past the too-large weekend houses moonshadowed by the lights of their drives.

She didn't have a key to the pool anymore. It was Neil's parents who'd bought a condo in the middle-class subdivision of this subdivision against the urbane and poor, to drink through retirement summers and be close to Liv and Neil and his wife of that time. Like everything else, the pool keys stayed in the house the day she and Jason packed her things and moved her to the apartment in Galena.

Maria left her sandals in the car and climbed the fence barefoot. It was eight feet, maybe, chain-link. The pressure of the metal put a dead ache through her big toes that sharpened with each release of the three or four steps of the climb. Presided as the first pain when she jumped from too high on the opposite side, to jarred knee and scratches across the callouses on her heels.

Liv, still leaning on the glass, stayed in the Cavalier until Maria opened the gate and came to fetch her. She was awake now but still limping on her mother's hip. The heavy white lights of the pool dampened the sky to blackish grays, when Maria switched them on. She looked up at the moon, a shredded white behind the clouds that came after the rain, and thought that, if a light organ were played right, even for a second, it would blight out the stars, and the pianist, for that time, would be enshrined in a world of her own creation— and for once it would be right, for the case alone that it was beautiful to her.

She took off her top, her bra, her pants and underwear. Liv watched her, staring at her mother's body emerging. Soft and pale and pretty. She stood there, over Liv, Athena in the floodlights, black hair over her eyes, pushed forward by the wind and helmeting her face from expression. She pushed her daughter into the water with one stiff arm and stood at the edge watching a moment before she dove into the water herself, over the little, struggling body—everything above them shimmering.

LONG WEEKEND

There isn't a single thing I've done, or experienced,
that's been even the least bit exciting.
— Grant Wood

This night Mary stayed late at the library for a Labor
Day celebration. It was just the staff, the three of them.
They ate cookies made by the director—snickerdoodles
—and drank soda too old to sell in the machine. They
talked about the patrons—the tall man with bangles on
his wrist who thumbs through *Guideposts* magazines
from four or five decades ago; the fourteen-year-old boy
once banned from the computers for looking up
pornography, who's now begun using them to search
the social media pages of his favorite actresses, their
nipples covered with pasties, his left hand shifting
fretfully over the top of his jeans; the woman who is
still searching for the book that will explain drinking
and driving laws, Connecticut, 1973.

Mary works forty minutes southwest of Dubuque,
forty north of Iowa City, in a town off the Wapsipinicon.
The river makes the town muggy at summer's end. She

braids her hair to keep stray strands from sticking to her eyelids, which inevitably they do, as now, while she walks circuitously home from work, from the party, pleased, if a bit stopped up with sugar and sugar. It must be seventy degrees, though it's near seven o'clock, and the bars she walks past are full of heated chatter.

The river below, while she walks through the park, over its slatted bridges, by its white oak and scrub pine, smelling of late summer green and decomposing in the loam, thick on itself, dead leaves on dead leaves that are not yet soil, the river is quiet but moving, as if in all directions. Another strand on an iris, hard to pull away.

Over the south end of the park, the sky is a contusion. Clouds striate horizon so that the sun, somewhere above, spreads from a perse into violets and pinks.

Mary lives in a brick house off Ford Street, north of the permanent awnings here, where families have celebrations—though, despite the fresh long weekend, none are here right now. Rather, here is the man in bangles, his blond hair falling between the boards of the table where he sleeps. She waves to him, wishing him awake, wanting to be recognized one more time before her three-day vacation. The feeling leaves, and she's almost content with watching the sparrows chase flies above the water.

The man in bangles catches up with her on Walworth Avenue. She's startled when he approaches, coming as he does with his long slow gait behind her.

"Ecclesiastes," he says. "You ever read that one?"

"No," she tells him, pulling her backpack to her shoulders. "What's interesting about it to you?"

"It's real interesting," he says. His bangles clank as he points back to the park. "The Mamas and the Papas wrote a song about it. You're too young to know the Mamas and the Papas."

"I know them," Mary says. She is still walking and he is too, getting ahead of her and stopping when she can't keep stride. "Mama Cass."

"Everything turn, turn, turn," he says, not quite singing, "And all that. A time for… you know that one?"

"I guess," she tells him. It sounds so familiar, but his voice is grainy. She can't parse the tune.

He turns abruptly towards her and says, without new enthusiasm, "Well, it's good stuff. You'd like it."

When she gets to her little brick house, her mother has supper nearly ready. She and her parents eat fettuccine pesto and listen to a CD of pieces by Brahms. Tomorrow, they'll drive into Iowa City to buy fresh curry leaves. It will have been a very exciting weekend.

BROKEDOWN PALACE

Ronnie Bleaker kept pinup girls tacked around his garage, between the top of the peg boards that showcased his tools and drywall where the walls met the ceiling. It was Iowa, summertime. Striker and I were thirteen, and because it was Iowa, we only ever saw cattle teats and glimpses of nipples through wet swimsuits and the occasional two-inch-by-two-inch bar calendar long-haul men kept in their trucks.

Ronnie was a machinist for Quaker Oats. That's what he said, and that made sense, but we never asked much about it. He was quiet and had hard hands with perpetual oil black around the cuticles. In the winter he wore jackets and blue jeans like the rest of us, but, from May to November, it was rare to see Ronnie Bleaker in anything other than camo pants and a cutoff T. He had little blue pen ink tattoos under his shoulders that read *Semper Fi* and his initials, pictures of the Buddha and a geisha in silhouette.

Ronnie wasn't any particular age to me. Old, I guess, like everyone who'd already lived through high school. He was, first, our first pot dealer. We hadn't worked our way up to anything dangerous, not to our knowledge. The pot was bad but we weren't conscious yet. Ronnie talked like magic and smelled like oatmeal, and motor oil. Looked like Sid Vicious reincarnate and taught us to roll trees, showed us how to repair our bicycles. That made him, as he said, "a purveyor of freedom, a Christ of life anointed in oil on the open road." We had no idea what that could mean, but it sounded like the sophisticate's version of dangerous, anarchy refined. Striker thought, in the way of boys, he might be specially blessed, he living two doors west of my house, so two doors closer to Ronnie Bleaker.

I'd wake up at nine or ten and get dressed and have some cereal. I'd knock on Striker's door and he'd come out. His dad would shout after us like some TV mother that he should be good and be home in time for supper. We'd walk our bikes to Ronnie's and he would be up already, in the garage, fiddling with his motorcycle like it was in need of constant repair.

We never saw the inside of his house, I don't think, or I didn't. It was a pale-yellow ranch, a little worse cared for than the others on our street. We didn't worry much about those things. We weren't interested in them. "Houses are not the tools of our momentum," Ronnie said. "You have to keep your eyes on the point where the road turns over the earth. Not the houses, not the horizon. You have to keep riding at the curve. The earth keeps turning. You'd run into anything else."

So that summer Striker and I kept riding, passed a hundred similar houses in our town, along the gravel roads and corn draws, by the girls we thought we were flirting with as we flirted and they rejected us.

My parents were high school sweethearts. My mother, a freshman when they started dating. My father, a sophomore, already an Eagle Scout and a starting halfback on the varsity football team, the Indians.

I was born in May that same school year. The following season, the high school let my father keep playing and allowed my mother to attend games with the understanding she sit amongst the adults and never wear my father's jersey and nurse me somewhere not visible from the stands.

My sister was born a year later. We both attended our parents' graduations in our grandmothers' laps and when, years later, we each student taught in Iowa City, we each encountered the parents of students who'd shared business classes with our father. That was in the late '80s and early '90s, mostly. But this was—my parent's short courtship and my own childhood—in a small town, in the Midwest, in the late 60's and in the '70s—which is the decade still most shaped for me.

Teenagers did worse things then than fuck a few times without condoms and keep the baby, the babies. They did worse things than start families young. They disappeared into the cities of the East and of the West and wrote home only for money to fund the cults they declared superior to the capitalist trash that supported them. They drugged others who unwittingly slept with them at concerts and in bar alleys. They stole from small store owners because they wanted to be as free as Abby Hoffman told them they were, someday, capable of being. They traveled the world to kill children in jungles scorched with DuPont chemicals. None of the naïveté left their older brothers lived by, carried in.

Among my earliest memories is one of watching the news with my father. He was twenty, maybe, or twenty-one—his draft number never came up. Protestors had bombed a University of Wisconsin science building, killing a young researcher, a father of three, inside. I look back at the warped panes now and odd litter scattered on the lawn and think, *Was it any wonder my parents were able to settle so easily into their life together, with its minor sins? To be at ease in themselves, in their work, in their homes, with my sister and me, bastards we were?*

Far back as I can remember Ronnie rode a black Indian with burgundy hubs. Burgundy so dark you had to stare at it going by to know your eyes hadn't played a trick in the sun. When we visited him, he would brag to us about cathouses. Wherever else he seemed to be going on that motorcycle—to a bar, to the shop, to the grocery store—cathouses were always his endpoint, what home was to our parents in the evenings, his place of refuge, his shelter from the storm. This was Iowa at a time when cathouses were nearly gone, a fond memory of middle-aged men and the daydreamed salvation of boys like Striker and me were becoming. A place folks knew you were going to go. You could say what you needed there and get it. And nobody judged you for that, and no one asked questions.

At the time still, and I think now, Striker and I didn't consider that summer as being about Ronnie Bleaker. We were young enough to have, between us, three or four preoccupations and no ambitions yet to relive or to be past what we'd lived through already. Young enough to be without suspicions, except maybe over Striker's father, who was a forgiving man but hopeful his son would become a doctor.

Striker did become a doctor, eventually, though a PhD in Philosophy and long after his old man died of a heart attack. We were eighteen when he died, early college. Night before the funeral, we rolled a joint and played "Box of Rain" off a recording I made at Alpine Valley. Realizing for the first time we could only forget what we'd repeated, we rewound that tape and played it again, and again. The words to ease us. Uncle Jerry's solo dropping water into our sorrow, each note just behind its feeling. That was in the future, though. Now it's in the past.

That summer, '79, time was still linear. And it was short. That's what we kept saying, like we knew what it meant, or what it had meant. That summer was about running around, searching for mythical, easy girls who would train on us before disappearing into Ronnie's cathouses, or, like men, accidenting casually onto some cathouse door. It was about music and anarchy. It was about being who we thought we were and never being judged.

The trouble with our attitude was there were, of course, no such girls, not single-minded and unabashed and lovely. Not at thirteen. Not older. There weren't women or girls desperate for us with our soft cheeks and cowlicks. And at some point we knew there weren't and we stopped wanting what wasn't, and the whole time we talked and talked about what we'd wanted without ever quite saying they weren't coming.

Ronnie Bleaker's house had a two-door garage. It stood out on our block because it made the house seem vaster. He had the Indian and a Chevy C-10 he drove around in the wintertime and to his job in Cedar Rapids. Ronnie was a pale man with a pale man's freckled tan. When the weather was nice, he'd leave the truck in the drive, working in the garage in the half dark with one door closed, whichever was farthest from the sun.

Striker and I always knew when Ronnie was home that way, and we nearly never took him by surprise. We'd come down the block at full volume singing "I Want to Be Sedated" or going on again about how great Raquel Welch looked in her wet dress in *Animal*, those long slits up the thigh.

When we arrived, Ronnie would be lying on his back with the Indian on a prop stand, unbolting the clutch in a yogic pose. Or he'd be squatting beside the bike, pulling off side plates and washing them in a basin of soap and water. Most times, he'd wait for us to come in and laugh and say, "Raquel Welch? Boy, you want to see a real pair of legs, you gotta get a look at Faye Dunaway. Goddamn *Chinatown* broke my heart."

Ronnie was never a punk kind of guy. His garage was always busy with the Dead, *Blues for Allah* mostly, and '60s rock & roll blues—The Stones, Janis Joplin, Dusty Springfield. He just played it, and because he was the adult, we tolerated it, liked it even, though I'd have never said so, even to myself. And Ronnie, he tolerated us, letting us talk, talking with us, all of us sharing a joint.

By the music, 1979 was a summer of loss and love. Near fourteen years into the relationship, my father tried to seduce my mother again, leaving the radio on during dinner in hopes of singing along with Roger Voudouris. The girls in our grade were meanwhile already crying into hairbrushes about how the loves they'd had had had hearts of glass—all that lost handholding. It was prescient, maybe, because, while Striker and I would abandon punk shortly after, it was years still before acid bands with their good vibes and love and honesty would sink into my sense of romance. I saw girls who were good-looking as something else, another class, and when a few of them, eventually, had the bad sense to keep company with me, I treated them like the fly-by-night daydreams I thought they might be.

In college, late in college. I spent seven years taking classes here and there, frying eggs, bartending, rushing cross-country to trip for a couple days watching the Dead at Red Rocks or in San Francisco. Late in college, the woman who would be my wife and after fifteen years leave me for another man, a friend. My girlfriend then, she was smoking pot with me on the back porch of a house we were renting. The house was white, vinyl-sided, and roofed green. You could smell the wet mold from the vinyl and the earthy old tar of the roof shingles fallen in the grass.

We'd been drinking beer all day. It was hot, August or September. The house was on the Iowa River, and it was humid but the breeze off the water cooled your arms, your cheeks, the curve toward your back where your hairline meets your neck. I asked her, "Maria, would you marry me?" No plan, no ring—I just said it and she put her hand on my thigh and said, "Yeah, I guess." She smiled.

"Alright," I said. "I see all the kids on campus and think maybe I'm not getting old enough."

"Not hell to be wrong," she said. "Just hell to be different."

"Yeah," I said, "I guess." Then I thought about it and took another drag. "Hell not to be yourself," I said.

She said, "That's another thing entirely." And she was right. Or at least I think she was, which is why I'm always going back to it.

Striker and I both took a shot at Carolyn Saunders, who wasn't the most attractive girl we knew but the most attractive girl we knew, our age, with enough attitude about her to be pursued. She had black hair she kept in a ponytail, low off to one side of her head. The side switched. She was ambidextrous—that was the joke, able to use her hands, Striker said, any way she chose.

We bumped into Carolyn at the grocery store and Striker whispered something into her ear: his secret, beside the baked goods and raisins. She laughed and he walked off and nothing else seemed to happen. I saw her about three days later, coming out of the laundromat and decided Striker had failed. I gave her his "use your hands" line. She was in a T-shirt and tight jeans washing had taken some of the blue off of. She was holding a basket of laundry still hot from the dryer. I was hopeful. I could have died.

Carolyn didn't care for either of us. So I tried the same line with Christine Simon, who wore a lot of white collared shirts and who Striker said was preppy. She was, but I rejected that notion after she made out with me behind the elementary school gym. When I tried again a week later, one of my hands went too far. Striker and I agreed on preppy after that.

He tried to start with Abby Collins. I thought she was ugly, too skinny, long-nosed. Now I see it, what was there, the body she was growing into. And I think she liked him, enough to put up with whatever he did, which I guess wasn't much. For the whole couple weeks they were together, I kept asking, "Did you get at it yet?"

He kept saying, "No, man," real quiet like he was serious, "we're, you know, warming up."

"So next time," I'd say.

"Maybe," he'd say. "I don't know."

And one time, I said "Maybe next time, we can see her together."

He said, "Maybe. I guess I'll think about it." If he kept seeing her after that he didn't mention it, and at some point it must have ended because, eventually, I would have known. That was all years ago, I don't wish it'd been different.

Once, a while after I kissed Christine Simon, Striker and I went over to Ronnie Bleaker's. I'd let a little air out of my front tire. I didn't need an excuse to see Ronnie, or even to tell him about Christine, but even when I thought about it, I started telling myself a story that made it bigger than it was. I guess I wanted Ronnie to be looking at something, and I wanted Striker to be looking at Ronnie, so when I gave them my big fish it would feel a little casual. Drift by into fact.

Striker and I walked the bike over to Ronnie's. On the one side of the garage, the dark side then, was a big green air compressor, with one of those dramatic gauges our fathers talked so much of blowing off into someone's skull who hadn't been watching the pressure rise.

Ronnie took the front tire off my bike and turned the compressor on. While it rattled and filled, he pulled out a tree and some chewing tobacco and talked a while about Cannonball Adderley. We just sat there smoking. Ronnie was playing the *In New York* album, kept pulling the needle back to hear Cannonball say, "You know, you get a lot of people who are supposed to be hip, you know, and they act like they're supposed to be hip—which makes a big difference, you see what I mean." While the horns started Ronnie kept talking through them, repeating that line, or "You know, hipness is not a state of mind, it's a fact of life." and once or twice landing on "You don't decide you're hip, it just happens that way, you see what I mean."

Sometimes, when he talked, Ronnie would tap his Skoal can against his hip in time with the music, and I remember thinking, that afternoon, as he pointed it at me, that that can between his fingers wasn't really an accusation. It was a circle his words turned on. You didn't really know where in the room they were falling, or if they fell at all.

"I felt up Christine Simon," I said.

"Don't know her," Ronnie said.

"She's preppy," Striker said.

"Striker's gonna fuck Abby Collins," I said, "maybe." I was feeling a little alienated and a little magnanimous. Course, truth told, I don't know why I said that.

"Shit," Ronnie said. "That compressor makes everything sound out of time." He took my tire and kept feeling around it with both hands. "How'd this sumbitch get so flat. You'd think there'd be a hole in here somewhere."

"Probably just a little one. Just can't hear it," said Striker.

"Probably," said Ronnie, "but I aint listening." He looked at the compressor gauge and put the nozzle to the tire. "Don't know her either. My advice is don't sleep with easy women. Penicillin can't fix everything."

"Abby isn't easy," Striker said.

"Doesn't matter," Ronnie said. He turned the compressor off. "Anyway, whatever you do, you have to learn to be careful and keep your mouth shut. Keep her name out of it anyhow."

"Yeah," Striker said.

Ronnie handed me back my tire and told me I should practice putting it on myself. So I did and Striker helped. "Should last you a day or two," Ronnie said. "If it's a leak, we'll know tomorrow.

"Yeah," I said. "That's right."

He said, "Boys, pussy aint everything.

"Right," Striker said.

"Right," I said.

"What the hell am I telling you for," Ronnie said. Cannonball was somewhere into "Gemini" finally. "Takes a man a long time to get that right. Can't tell people some things. They got to burn it down personally."

There was a pool in town but from noon to two it closed so that all the kids would go home for lunch. Then there was an hour of swim class no one over twelve was allowed in. Striker liked to swim. I didn't, but I liked to watch the swimmers. Some days we'd go to the pool. Some days we'd stay at Ronnie's too long. It'd be one o'clock or whatever it was by the time we left, so we'd ride our bikes up north of town, to the river.

The river wasn't a river really, you couldn't really swim in it. It was a creek with river in its name, that we ran through barefoot catching tadpoles as they splayed away, that we wrestled in the tallgrass beside, that we heckled the silence of with Striker's portable radio. We only got three stations there and liked the anarchy of the noise as much as complaining about AM talk programs and country twang.

We used to light up and talk about forming a band, but neither one of us could sing and we both wanted to be the drummer. Striker would sit beating rhythms out on the grass with old corn stalks or cattails. I'd sit with him, thinking about lyrics and, mostly, coming up with band names. "Velo City," I said once.

"What?" said Striker.

"For the name of our band," I said. "Velo City, like velocity but you break it."

He said, "I don't know, man." He kept drumming away until one of his cattails broke. He got up and picked it up and kept playing, holding the plush end this time. "Velo City."

"It's fast," I said.

"But it takes you a long time to realize what you're saying," he said.

"That's anarchy," I said.

He said, "Yeah."

He got the idea after that that Velo City ought to have a sports team—that was the joke, that was the band. He formed the Velo City Wailers in high school, with a couple other guys, while I started playing football and wrestling. The band fell apart a couple years later when Striker started listening to the Talking Heads. The rest of the band was still on Dylan and couldn't see the connection.

At the start of college, Striker re-formed with a junior math professor who had a voice like Mike Gordon. It was a band of just the two of them they named Velo City. Their first album was called Zeno. The cover had a drawing of a runner and a tortoise divided into lanes by a series of arrows. Nobody got the joke but it was a solid album, a Phish kind of album—quieter though, more focused, with an arc. Hippies dug it and so did the stoner kids who weren't hippies, who dropped quaaludes and listened to Brian Eno and Joy Division.

Striker sold it out of record shops in Iowa City and the Quad Cities and in Des Moines. Somebody who knew somebody must have stopped into one of them passing through, because somewhere, two or three years into school, this publicist called Striker up to offer him an opener spot on a New Riders show. It was an incredible gig, but I was disappointed even Striker didn't meet the band, not for more than a handshake. They liked him though, I guess, and he pulled a few more gigs out of it.

He and the junior professor both quit school to go on tour. At some point, the publicist renamed them Velocity Zero and at some other point the junior math professor decided he liked New York and stayed there to play as a studio guitarist.

Striker traveled around for a while, with a new group, named Again, the Velo City Wailers. Some of his friends from that time said things were going well, that by all accounts he'd really made it. I don't know. I didn't hear much from him. Never asked.

For a year or two, he would just pass through. He sent me cassette tapes of singles before he released them. Then one day he came back to Iowa to stay, with no explanation other than that everyone confused him for Bob Marley, who he wasn't, and he was worn down by all the cities.

We were always welcome at Ronnie's, it didn't matter when. We could just wander in bullshitting, and he'd be ready for us, pleased. We'd come in and talk about nothing or I'd talk at them about nothing, while Ronnie played the Kinks and Striker watched the girls smile from the wall. Eventually, I'd ask Striker for the time. He'd say noon or whatever, and Ronnie would make a joke.

"Nooner," he'd say, "and no one. Difference between them just the space, and another r."

"Whoa," Striker would say.

"Whoa," I'd say back, and once, "Hey wait. That doesn't make sense. There isn't an r in no one."

"Smart boy," said Ronnie Bleaker, "but you're wrong."

It was all nonsense and all fine like that, except one time. Striker had his radio out and we came up on the house, excited we'd caught the college station from Iowa City. They were playing the Velvet Underground, "The Black Angel's Death Song." Striker kept saying, "Man," real breathy, and I kept saying, "Whoa, whoa." It blew our minds.

"What is it with you and this shit?" Ronnie was still behind the east side door. Already stoned, the suddenness of his, that third voice between us, caught me unprepared.

Striker, though, was never surprised by anything. "What shit?" he asked.

"The Sex Pistols, the Ramones, Patti Smith, all that shit." One of Ronnie's tools rang, a wrench set down maybe, with a high staccato shot. Striker was jaunting at the door, the way lovers who've been apart sort of gallop in each other's direction. It was a funny thing about Striker, that he could go whole days without saying a word, then rush into conversation when it really mattered to him. Anarchy mattered to him, it was worth expostulating on, defending.

"It's great," he said.

Ronnie stepped out, wiping his hands on an old red paisley handkerchief. Striker ran square into his chest. "This is what I mean, man. This shit just gets you riled up. There's no finesse."

"Fuck finesse," said Striker. Ronnie was holding him by the forearms and Striker shoved off. "The world is fucking burning, Ronnie."

"What are you talking about, kid. You haven't even seen the world."

"I've seen more than you think," Striker said. The breeze was up, filling Striker's sleeve and pinning it to his arm and filling it again. Ronnie hovered over him, as tall as he was, as hard and dark-veined, like he'd really fight a thirteen-year-old over, I realized, I wasn't sure what. I realized my friend and this man who spent whole mornings with us were both, in that moment, full of complete bullshit.

I read somewhere, some interview I guess, that after the Sex Pistols dropped him, Sid Vicious declared, "I was the only guy with any bit of anarchy left." He moved to New York, did heroin, and murdered Nancy, probably. I don't know when I realized—you have to be stoned to realize a thing at once—that my life wouldn't have any of that anger in it.

I used to be jealous of city kids with their street smarts and indifference, their casual wisdom about the dark heart of humankind. In my late twenties, I'd still only visited cities, real cities, with their slim streets and colored lights and buildings to block the sun. Briefly, Maria and I tried Chicago, then San Francisco.

In a mad rejection of ourselves, we fluttered for a someplace else early married life might take us. We wanted to be, we learned, who we'd always been, to our earliest memories, both of us smalltown, private, bursting inside ourselves with chatter and lust. We couldn't even pretend to be as angry as that someplace else required—or I couldn't.

Maria and I married about a week and a half after I graduated, enough time to party and sleep it off and start the party over again. She wore a white dress and I wore a tuxedo, but to the last day we joked about eloping in blue jeans, making the preacher give us the *I dos* with both of us shirtless.

I had, by then, been spending most of my time with a half dozen jazz musicians who'd chosen Iowa City to study in for all the reasons you'd expect. Maria didn't like any of them, but three stood for me. Striker was my best man, though that was just after the heyday of Again, the Velo City Wailers. With Striker back in Iowa, we saw each other more often but he studied mostly, and slept, since he'd put his ambition to use.

The wedding was nice. My mother still says that, to no other purpose maybe than to make me think the celebration was worth its ending. And, truth told, it was.

Maria and I lived pretty happily for ten or so years. I went to work at a school and got bored and we moved, for a minute, to two cities. We came back to the rural Midwest, where she taught piano lessons then took over her father's restaurant, while I taught English at a nearby high school. We drank at night. She read books aloud while I cooked. We got drunk and listened to Jerry Garcia, or Beethoven, or Thelonious Monk, or Widespread Panic—it depended on the night and the vibe.

At some point, she thought we ought to drink a little less. She decided it was getting to the time we should start taking ourselves seriously. And, honestly, I had been. I was doing what I'd wanted to be doing, exactly that. My back ached. I'd developed more pains than I'd hoped for, but I was getting what I'd intended. It was a long strange trip and I was loose and enjoying it.

I don't know that the right things have stayed in my mind, or that what's stayed has been accurate. Fine by me if it isn't. Why dwell on progress and holding like the whole of my life was some capacious desk drawer, a hall closet full of perfect little memories waiting for me to turn back to teenage anarchy, to metamorphose into Proust or Flaubert, better.

The truth is I am hardly literate. The truth is that's fitting, because all the rubber bands and bottle caps, a madeleine and letters from past lovers, and the pencils

I've stolen from school, they don't make the time lived. These exercises in being what you were, in being what you'll be to fight it back, what you've seen but haven't been. I forget and forget but my body's lived it all, and all told, that can't be all, but it's what I've known, and have been pretty pleased.

It was August or getting to be August, 1979. I was thirteen and so was Striker. We were out at the river that day practicing for our band, conducting interviews with a dismissiveness we'd learned from Lou Reed and Dylan, the first greats of rock and pissing. I'd hold a microphone fist to Striker's lips and say, "Why do you act like this?"

He'd say, "Because nothing matters, man."

I'd say, "You can't really believe that, can you?"

He'd say, "How can I believe anything?"

"I don't know," I'd say. "But—"

"You might just be where you're at," he'd say, "Then you're where you're at. Maybe you think you have to be going somewhere, and the earth's turning either way."

"Man, what are you talking about?" We were thirteen. We would laugh. That day we were laughing the whole way home. We were almost there, just a mile or so from home, laughing.

My father was working on a house, along the road on our way back. He was enclosing a porch before the summer ended. We saw his truck and stopped off, and he was pleased to see us, saying, "Boys," like he did when he was happy. Like you turning up was the only thing that could have made his day better.

I asked for money. We were always gathering his cash for weed and cans of chew, which, back then, collected in the backs of our closets like little unused silos. We never spoke about it. More than the weed it got us high and we didn't want to admit that that scared us.

We talked about nothing with my father. We were laughing when we left, my father laughing behind us. I rode ahead, and Striker's front tire picked up a nail and flattened. He called after me and I came back and we walked that final mile, dusk coming over us the colored-sand way it does in flatland Iowa. We'd intended to eat at Striker's house, and smoke after. But Ronnie's garage was open and there was the excuse of the flat tire.

The sun had come down so that everything turned that gray-blue. That's how you know the world is round, I thought. If the sun got behind you on a flat earth, you wouldn't see any light, except over the edges of yourself. I thought, you're not that big, that can't be true. I thought, Maybe the world is flat. Maybe that's what happens at the Northern Lights. I thought, It doesn't matter. I thought, You have to know something. Then, I thought, maybe not.

Ronnie didn't hear us come up. He was on the garage floor, lying on his back on a piece of cardboard. He'd strung a light across the room that showed the geography of his cheekbones and jaw. Normally, the chrome exhaust pipes ran parallel the bike. Something had struck the lower pipe and peeled it back at a ragged angle, the way I've often imagined landmines and mortar shells shred limbs. Like a surgeon, with a pair of tin snips, Ronnie was cutting the waste away, focused but inexact. He was cursing to himself.

I said, "What the fuck happened, Ronnie?"

He said, "Fuck man, how you guys doing?" He propped himself up with his arms winged back. "Fucking bullshit on the highway, man. Something must've fallen off some truck. I didn't even see what this shit was. But it was right over this hill and I was passing a semi. Fucking lucky it didn't toss me, man, you know what I mean, but it sure as shit fucked my exhaust."

"Glad you're cool," Striker said.

"Yeah," I said, realizing then that I ought to say something comforting.

"Fuck man," he said, "yeah. Anyway, it's good to see you guys, man. My hands are so fucked up from the jolt, I can't get this shit off. I got to replace the pipe, but 'til then I can't be dragging it."

Ronnie asked the two of us to lie down. Striker held the pipe end and I got the tin snips. I cut at the metal, straight as I could with the curve of the blades. Ronnie held the light for us. He was squatting down, chinaman style, the way he must have in the Marines, the way I imagine him, his helmet hung on a pole for show and the light in one hand, held way up, pointing down.

I was fucking it up, I knew. I wanted it to look good, even if it was temporary, but the metal was stiffer than I thought it would be and the tin snips more oily. When I reached around, the cuts from the back bowed in and when I came from the front to even it out, I took off more than I meant to and the meet was a jagged sliver.

Ronnie didn't say anything, no instructions, no caution. After a few more cuts, I got frustrated trying to take the sliver off—I'd made three or four more in the meanwhile—and asked Striker if he wanted a go. He said, "Sure, man. Hold this."

And Ronnie said, "No." He said, "Neil, man, you got to do this. You got to commit."

It was like getting drunk and wandering into a palmistry shop. Like you maybe believe it and you know you shouldn't and you forget it right after but can't sleep. I looked up at him, Ronnie. He had that one hand way up. I couldn't see anything but the yellow light and his outline and the blue asterisks of streetlights glinting off his tools at the edge of my vision. The light hurt my eyes. I pinched them with my thumb and forefinger. The oil on my hands stung. I sat up and rubbed my eyes with the back of my wrist. I was tearing up, getting enough water going to wash it away. And it was like there just wasn't enough in me.

Ronnie was squatting there. Cock out, holding the light, stroking himself. Hand slick, flickering with oil. Even in the dark, with my eyes hazed, I could see it. I said, "Striker, man, we got to go."

We got up and went. Ran home. Left our bikes in his driveway. Never said a word, never spoke about it. That's all there was.

That was the end of a short summer. It had gone on like summers always do. I am a teacher and a lost boy. These summers aren't all I've ever known, but they are what I wish for most. When the weather is warm, I can play. Why would I care to do anything else?

I'm decades into pain. During college, when I was twenty-three or twenty-four, I slipped a disc playing rugby and three or four surgeries haven't fixed it. Not entirely. There are hours, days even, when I wake up and it's warm and I feel as loose and agile as when I was thirteen, but inevitably I move and the sharpness of the pain's return is enough to make me wish it'd never left. I drink and I dip, I smoke when I can. My doctor tells me it doesn't help but since my aches can't be fixed, I prefer pleasant medicine.

My daughter, Liv, was hard to hold when we first had her. I hadn't planned for her, and never prepared. It was before the first surgery. She didn't sleep, so we didn't sleep, and when she slept my muscles were so sore I stayed up. Vodka helped, with Vicodin. It eased them while I was drunk.

For me, that story's not a tragedy. I saw the late evening of a hundred sunsets over Iowa with their chalkdust clouds and hues of red. After, rising and gliding out I wander'd off by myself, / In the mystical moist night-air, and from time to time, / Look'd up in perfect silence at the stars.

You'd like to think you were heading in a direction, I guess because you don't ever see the world spin, except in globes. What you live is just the clouds passing over at a given speed and the sun coming one way, leaving the other. You never see the sun really. A passing glimpse. You can't study it without spotting your eyes and so it could be, just maybe, a different star every time. Like a country road sees one pickup truck and then another. Same pale fellow in a mesh ballcap, or might as well be. But he doesn't run around the earth— you know he can't. And the next fellow tips his brim, maybe blows a kiss, drives a motorcycle, maybe a van.

DAYS BETWEEN

It's unusually warm for the middle of May, and muggy. Yesterday drizzled grim. Today, the sun hangs low and yellow in an open sky. In the wood behind his house, the tree leaves seem to have grown. The limbs of black walnuts hang heavy under their weight. Sunlight glints through still-wet clusters of leaves, in stained glass patterns. Neil Kenning is reminded of church—and why not—for nowhere else is he closer to divinity.

A lionish spring. Temperatures have leapt in the past few days, from highs in the thirties to lows in the seventies. Neil wonders if the long cold and quick change will have kept the morels from growing, large and yellow, as he likes them. Then again, it is not too cold or too hot for morels, and a few steps into his hunt, he is imagining trash bags so full they can't be tied closed, honeycombs peeping out bag tops.

There is a fallen birch three, four acres into the wood, and, in Neil's opinion, only one way to it. He hasn't much else to do but daydream. Liv is with her mother. It is Maria's birthday. Nina, her grandmother, is taking the two of them to Dubuque—for an eight-dollar meal and ten dollars down the penny slots, if Neil knows Nina. So Neil is doing what he wants to do: getting outside, stumbling over brambles, hunting down the evening's meal, or this small part of it. He is communing with Nature, with the early mayflies and ferns over the felt green moss of still water, its sparkling flits of light escaping.

When he spots the birch, Neil begins to walk with care, laying feet—trying—where oak leaves haven't fallen to the forest floor and spring dried into crisps. Over the years, jokes that morels are like fish have begun to feel factual. In some simple, ridiculous way he believes mushrooms, the best ones, have a means to hear and will disappear if he plods too heavily. They'll go skittering off or recede into loam.

This is confirmed when he gets on hands and knees and begins to lift the edge of the birch, cracks a branch, only to find his haul, his trash bag loads, have disappeared into the forest, into the earth, under the cover of bloodroot and mayapples, leaving three small mushrooms to fend for themselves.

Neil pulls a plastic bag from his back pocket, puts the mushrooms in and walks on into the forest. He sneaks up on a patch beneath a black cherry. Happens on several hiding beneath a thorn thicket. He terrifies a squirrel, two killdeer, who wing off declaring their kildeer threat, when he trips over a maple root, falling and catching himself, wrenching a shoulder. Neil grunts into the wood. There's a fledgling where he falls, its skeleton melded to mud.

He gets up, pulls mud bits from his blue jeans and the heels of his palms. He twists his fanny pack to his front and takes out a small Ziploc baggie of Vicodin, swallows three with a swig of water from his Nalgene.

His back and shoulder pain him, as they always do, that permanent ache of biting something cold and sweet. And discomfort him in an unknown fashion, as if the shoulder has been yanked apart and the arm can't make its socket.

The thought of that new separation makes him stomach-sick. Minor accidents like this strike a sense in him he might actually be falling to pieces. Because, as it turns out, at least for Neil, the claim that disability strengthens some other part of one's self has never proven true.

When he busted his spine in his twenties, slipped a disc, L3, it changed his life in ways he couldn't have imagined—even if he'd been imagining pain. He'd never realized how little he relied on his strong side. He'd had to give up rugby and wrestling, though he tried to keep them up. His bartending became slow. At least in the first weeks of convalescence, he'd had to set glasses on the bar or flat under the taps to pour them. Patrons complained of long waits and pints half full of foam. Scott, the owner, was too loyal to fire him, or knew, with his ex-wife no longer keeping the books, the bar was on its way to closing. Why fight it through with Neil who seemed to be closing too?

Neil raises the aching shoulder to hang its arm behind his head, stretching fingers and extending the hand as he searches for a place things can fall into. He tucks a plug of Skoal in the back of his mouth, between his cheek and jaw. There's a sore tooth there. The tobacco makes it ache and throb and numbs it finally in a way he finds cathartic, distracting.

He considers going back to the house, cooking the two dozen or so tiny mushrooms he's collected. But going home will only draw his mind to his solitude and the shoulder. Livie will be back tonight. He won't be able to hunt this long or this deep in the wood tomorrow. There is nothing more likely to scare a morel than the chatter of a child.

He takes another Vicodin, two, and walks up the canyon slope, out of his own land. He has no fences but knows where he is. An inexplicable hump of grass, sloping gently if starkly from the earth. There are glacial erratics well north of here, but this land was untouched by the last ice age and this hill is not erratic. It is a burial mound, belonging to the DNR, rather, protected on property the DNR has claimed. Small compared with some, but stunning in its smallness, round against the water-carved hills surrounding it, alike and of another kind. Neil has seen it, many times. When old Iowa friends come to visit, hunt deer, he sometimes brings them up this way on the pretense of showing them the land's edge. They rave about the queer, spiritual feelings they experience near the mound.

Neil does not have them, these feelings—not about the mound. It's as if only your own gods may come to you, as though to trespass on the gods of others is the only great sin. He is hard pressed to believe in death, in signifying death. Instead he thinks of the world in perpetual motion. When a tree falls, a mushroom grows beneath its trunk. When Neil dies—anyway, we're all gonna die—he wants not to be buried in a way that marks his passing: not for his family, not for Liv, not for anyone. Neil Kenning would like to fall in the forest and be consumed and grow again as a mushroom.

He sits down off the mound-side and drinks from his Nalgene and spits. He leans back on a hillette and looks at the sky, the forest canopy. A breeze makes his forehead feel moist, cool. He takes another Vicodin. Somewhere a limb snaps as an animal moves in the brush. Somewhere a tree creaks, nudged by the wind in the canopy. Neil's shoulder aches but less so when he settles back against the grass. With his good arm he pulls out the Skoal and tosses it spattering into the wood. He relaxes. His mind is clear. His breath is easy.

He sleeps, and when he sleeps he dreams, and in his dream he wakes, still resting, on the mound now, and he is melded to the mound, as if a patch of sod raised by winter ice and in the spring melt laid again just away from its former place. The air remains warm, damp. Dew drops stick to his leaves of grass. The sky above him is a pastel blue, and out of the corner of his vision he sees storm clouds, violet-blue and tinged with a hue of granite. He hardly thinks of moving. The sod lies still. Neil Kenning lies still, waits for the rain to wash him to wherever he will be.

While he waits, a man walks by in steel-toed boots. He steps on Neil, who wants to cry out but hasn't the voice. So his pain reaches tendrils down roots and little white flecks of loam that smell rich and alive. They send the pain across the topsoil, down and down and down, into the limestone and mantle, and the pain is gone, so the man.

There is silence, then thunder. Neil counts seconds to see how close the lightning's come, and, as he gets it, thunder rumbles through him with a shock, and he's forgotten, and it begins again. It doesn't matter. It begins again. What can he do but sit, wait, sit? He waits and sits and waits and sits, weighted down by the gravity of the earth, wetted leaves waving limply in the wind.

In the distance, at the edge of his sight, a woman walks in front of a cluster of leaves, through which he is watching the moving storm. She is nude, her whole body freckled with the little tan spots pale women get when they've been too long in the sun. Her hair, long and black. Her body, long and thin. Her fingers, her arms hang low and twig-like. They move little, though he sees the joints and bones when they do, brushing the outsides of her thighs.

Neil waits. He lies as she walks towards him. He sees behind her the storm. She looks forward, to the mound or just beyond it. Her eyes have the dark gray and tan immobility of aged bark. Her movements are steady, delicate, as if directed by wind, and while the urge to speak with her strikes him, it passes strangely and without regret. She reaches the mound and stands above him, looking out and away. She hasn't come here for the mound. The woman looks down, smiles, her teeth white, misaligned as crossing limbs. She has in her that peculiar beauty of being without self-consciousness.

The woman lies beside him, on her side, and one long arm stretches sweepingly over his grass. Turning on her stomach she takes a single blade between thumb and forefinger. She eyes it for what seems an eternity, but is only the time it takes for the storm to catch them.

Her skin against him soft, almost weightless. "You shall possess the good of the earth and sun, (there are millions of suns left)..." The rain is fast and swift. It falls heavy into uncombed hair, onto her face, dots bark-grained eyes, and melts her whole into him, he into her, the two of them into the soil, the mantle, down.

When they wake, decades later, they are mushrooms in the dark beneath a fallen birch, with a streak of light knifing through the paper bark. And they are alone in the world, these mushrooms, staring out into everything they are part of.

LIES, DAMNED LIES, AND STATISTICS

A REAL DRAG PRINCESS

Two-month chip, steps 4 through 9. Not linear, where you're at. He had a headphone over one ear. He was playing along to a backing track of "Recorda-Me" on his Walkman, playing his tenor sax alone in Dupont Circle, standing in front of the fountain in front of the nude who is pulling her hair up with one hand in a way that is luxurious but not quite sexual. This would have been the summer of '93. It wasn't long after he'd moved to Washington from NYC. It was Monday, Pride Week.

His name was Jason. He'd graduated from Iowa a semester later than was expected, gone straight to the Big Apple after Christmas to make it in a real New York combo. That was the plan, though he'd spent most of his time drinking up savings while he sat and listened to bands whose players were well beyond him—in attention, in talent.

He'd seen Benny Green once in a jazz club in Harlem, bumped into Benny in the bathroom while they were both washing their hands. Benny saw his case on the floor, asked if he wanted to sit in.

"Yeah, man. I'd love that. That would be—that would be—great." Jason dried his cheeks with a paper towel, tried to stiff-limb a look like sober.

"Cool, man. Cool," Benny said. He smelled sour, earthy, of fresh burned weed, and something about that fact left Jason weak, immobilized. Here was this guy, a legend already, at—like—thirty, stoned as hell and playing his ass off. Jason was only seven or eight years younger, five or six beers in. But drunk or sober, he wasn't sure he could have gotten on stage with Benny Green and not embarrassed himself. He walked out the bathroom, onto the street. And it was gone—just like that—that chance, that dream.

Before the end of February, his graduation cash, the five hundred dollars his parents had given him to get started, was burned up. He'd taken a job at a bagel shop down the block from his sublet on the north end of Brooklyn, off the odd, quiet park space between Greenpoint and Williamsburg.

The job was convenient. He could spend nights at jazz joints in the Village and, when they closed around two or three, hop to the shop and heft forty-pound bags of flour into their giant mixing bowls. He would work 'til noon, sleep 'til six. Get up, practice. Be at a club by half past nine. Listening. Always listening. The dream was gone, not dead. He was sure he'd hear it come back. The rest, just temporary.

Assisting a baker is pretty menial labor. For a while, no one said shit about him coming in half-lit. Back in Iowa City, almost two decades later, it's hard to say anything about that time with much certainty, but he's sure he wasn't the only one tipsy in the kitchen, yeast mixed with wheat flour, cheap hops in all their nostrils.

Jason has found that life and music are both like Einstein's train, never exactly static. But—fake it 'til you make it—it's easier to understand them that way, the changes as pictures of the ever-shifting never was.

He'd rather it wasn't, that it hadn't been. Maybe most of it. But it happened. He's working on apologies, and you have to know what you've done.

So, he imagines the end of his first stay in New York contained in this moment: he staggers into the bakery one morning after hearing the Vanguard Orchestra, head still pulsing from the driving beat of the encore and shots of whiskey done with a lonely businessman from Seattle who saw his Selmer and assumed he was some sort of understudy to the band.

It was the end of March. Rent was late. The air sodden in a way that suited his haze. To this day he feels a hot shame at how the memory fades in and out in alcoholic waves. It isn't made better by anticipation.

What he is sure of is the pungent scent of sourdough and garlic baking in large Maytag ovens. His boss, a fat man in a navy-blue apron, saying, "Fuck, you think you can turn up an hour late?" The difficulty of hoisting a flour sack making him sick, straight into a mixer.

You come to learn that sidewalks are the way deserts are often described: searing hot in the shine of day, biting cold in the shade of buildings, with no sun to reflect. Cold soon, too, after they've been covered by your body. Though worst is the contrast of putting hands on warm cement in a drizzle wind, becoming sick with the confusion of temperatures.

This can be mediated. There are yesterday's newspapers to be plucked from trash cans beside unopened stands. There are cardboard boxes, bound in bundles, on curbs—on Wednesdays in your neighborhood.

For the first couple weeks after you've lost your job, been ousted from your apartment, then from the apartments of the two loose friends you made at that now lost job, you will have the illusion you are able to carry your bedsheets with you until this all gets sorted. The illusion you can carry everything you cared enough about to drag halfway across the country: pictures with the Maladies band, books of Emerson and Hesse, Ellison and Kierkegaard, a dank pipe, a singing bowl. But you will find, at some point, you can't even carry your pride. Though you will try, never telling anyone, never even calling home when you have the change.

Jason stayed in New York through mid-May, practicing standards for tips and eating two-day-old bagels from the trash bags coffee shops reserve for the homeless. By the end of that first month his energies were drained. He couldn't spend more time than he had already wondering if he'd had to leave his apartment, had to leave the apartments of his friends, which complaints were valid and for which he should apologize, change.

Didn't matter. Not then. He knew he'd never say I'm sorry. They should move past it. That's how he'd thought arguments ended. But, where was he going to see them—his landlord, his boss, his friends—to end an argument? The Big Apple, big pond, doesn't need your reconciliations. You go on keeping yourself warm with cardboard and bottle shots. They would never even think of you, except to fill sound from time to time, say, *I wonder what happened to him.*

Him, Jason. That's the lesson. He hitched to D.C. where he thought the weather would treat him better. Which was true in late-May, into June. The breezes seemed gentle. The sun was out a little longer each day. Something about having new streets to wander, new places to explore, free museums to walk through—when the security guards would let him in—made Washington seem like a strange vacation, a blend of camping and urban adventure.

The tenor sax was popular beyond all reason in the District that summer. Apart from the Hill itself, where Federal cops chased him off—District cops didn't give a damn—he could play most streets unbothered. Clinton was still settling in. Knickknack vendors sold Arsenio Hall shirts from their street-side trailers. The power-suited men in Georgetown and K Street, near the White House, would drop fives, sometimes tens, in his Folgers can.

Those months, humid as they were, were the best of his sixteen on the street. From late-May, nearly through August, Jason was able to put himself up in a hostel on 11th Northwest, and the wriggly, live-in manager, a hippie girl from rural Wisconsin, didn't boot him for staying too long or missing a day's rent, and sometimes kissed him in the kitchen against the sink when the other guests had gone to bed—never before and never more, though he tried. He'd reach up under her shirt and thumb her belly button. She'd take his wrist, pull it away before he moved in any farther.

"You're beautiful," she'd say and walk off with slow, deer-step motions in her hips.

In those months, he didn't count money or strategize where to play. Didn't have to. He could do stupid things, like blowing alone in the middle of Dupont Circle, a headphone over one ear, while old men played clock chess behind him.

30 days—first 30, last 30—30 in front of you's the hardest 30. 60 days. He's got 60 days. His name is Jason. Never thought it'd be different, never wanted it erased. Jason. Hi Jason.

He remembers, or has decided for the sake of memory, that he was in the middle of "Recorda-Me," leading from the B^b major to the B^b minor of the A^b ii-V, when a falsetto voice began asking, "Excuse me? Excuse me?" repeatedly, in time, back a quarter step off the beat.

In those early days of being on the street, Jason held to the pretense he was providing something important, even innovative, to the city of D.C., that interrupting his performance for any fool who decided to talk at him was a disservice to everyone who could hear.

Channel Keith Jarrett: the people who get the music don't interrupt. The people who interrupt want to be thought of as people who get the music—usually. Or think of themselves as musicians—worse.

The voice insisted, then came into view, backdropped by hedges in the swiftness of a blink: a six-foot-three or six-foot-four, barrel-chested Black man in a skin-tight V-neck T-pink—and three-inch heels—

matching. Jason didn't even bother to resolve. Left a sharp nine dangling above the rooks and queens. Fingered in his pocket to stop the backing track. Pulled headphones over neckstrap. "What can I do for you?" he asked.

The man's cheeks were high. His mascara thick. What remained of his hair was stretched sparse with sweat and aluminum clips that glinted as he swayed, posing in imagined frames. When he stopped, momentarily, Jason could see, through glimmers of sun, red scabs along the front of his scalp where a wig, he guessed, had rubbed the skin raw.

"Hey," said Jason, just to fill the rest.

"Hi," the man said, hand out to be kissed. "I'm Lizbeth Princess." This soft and in crescendo, "I'm a drag queen. I work at IBM. I don't mean I do drag at IBM. Naturally. I dance down at the Madam's Organ. You don't know that place. Nice boy like you. It's down by the Zoo, in Adams Morgan. Big surprise, right?" Lizbeth pulled her hand back, threw an arm forward, elbow first.

"I know that joint," he lied.

"Then you've seen me," said Lizbeth. "I love it there. I love to dance to the blues bands. That's why I came to you. It's so empty out here. I heard you—I love the sax. I love to dance to the sax. And musicians are cool. You're cool, right? You're not going to hurt me?" She clutched the dark purse she had dangling from an elbow, took a step back, large pecs tensed, veins visible over the musculature of her arms.

"I don't understand," he said. He held the tenor forward, as if its brass facts were an answer.

"I'm a cross-dresser. You never know. It's pretty safe up here, all the gays—but some places are awful. Across the Anacostia. I can't walk over there. That's why I stopped. I'm in a real bind. I just came from this corporate gig I did with my friends, Butter Scotch, Barbie Wire. Over on U Street. It's Pride Week. You know that, cute boy like you. We were raising money for AIDS. Research, I mean. Naturally. We made better than twenty-five grand at this dinner we performed at. It was two hundred dollars a plate. Can you believe that? Anyway, I was flirting with this guy. A cute little redhead, like you—a little older. And so everyone is gone when I leave, and when I get out to my car, I realize I locked my keys in there." Her words out, Lizbeth breathed hard relief, threw herself forward, arms slumped to a bow.

"I don't really know a mechanic," said Jason. "I don't own a car. Look for a payphone, I guess?" He put the Selmer to his lips, ran a diminished pattern, waited for Lizbeth to leave.

She came close instead, held his shoulder with one deft hand, let the hand fall, nails scratching lightly down his back—up again, down, back up—leaning gently to let her nails reach his coccyx. Electric strings resonated over his spine, and in. He brought the pattern to the tonic, stopped. Stared off towards nowhere, he imagines, the way a dog does when you pet it by surprise.

"Please, honey. I'm in a bind."

"I dig," he said. "I'm sorry. It's just—this is how I make my money."

"That's what you think this is?" Her hand between his shoulders, Lizbeth shoved hard away. "Because I'm a

Black man and a faggot? I come down here looking for help. I don't need money, honey. I make eighty thousand dollars, *a year*. Eighty thousand, at I-B-M."

"It's hard to go around looking like I do without getting the shit kicked out of you. You dig? Especially in the nigger districts. You *dig*?" She reached her hands up as if to plead with the sky. Palms turned in, she let them fall in vase-shaped outline. "I'm just looking for somebody to go with me and wait while my tow comes. I don't want to get my ass kicked by some gang bangers after some coke." Lizbeth held that image: hands before her, thick chest raised.

"Listen." Jason said. "I didn't mean anything. People come by, they bother me for cash. It's out in the open. You called a locksmith? It's daylight. It's a ways to U Street, right? You call now, walk over there, your tow'll probably be there for you. Hang out, take a cab in twenty minutes if you're scared."

"Come here, honey." Lizbeth said. She drew him in by a hip, wrapping one arm behind him, slipping a hand across his sternum, under his horn. "I didn't mean to go off on you. It's hard sometimes, you know."

"It's cool," he said. "Really, we're cool." She moved his sax to one side, drew fingernail tips across his body in curlicues, over a thigh, his zipper.

"Man," he said, "I'm flattered—."

"Oh, honey," Lizbeth said, a deep nasal purr. There were pedestrians in the distance, their T-shirts bright against brick buildings. Jason could almost hear their talk, see the sides of their eyes glancing over topiary.

Of all the things he did outside in those days, he wonders why this moment makes him feel most judged, most encased. Why two decades before bottom, he couldn't meet it, even say now if he was sober. He held Lizbeth's wrist. Pushed her down on himself so her hand lay under his crotch. She tried stirring his testicles with slow, precise motions of fingers over denim.

He got half-hard, the sharp teeth of his zipper bit a side where her wrist pressed against him. He doesn't know if it was doubt or pleasure. She took it in her hand, and he gripped her wrist tighter.

"It's okay," she said, and went on, squeezing and letting go. One hand holding him, the other, on a hip, holding him up.

"It's okay." Her thumb pressed against him, her fingers drew balls to the shaft. He let it happen. Jason. Let it happen to him, Jason. He was powerless over alcohol. His life had become unmanageable. He's trying not to think that he asked for that. Knows even that's an excuse.

Lizbeth cupped his balls, bunched his jeans either side of the pleat. Her thumb went on rubbing, now a little, and a little more now, a little again. It had been so long since someone had touched him. He was almost there. So fast. He closed his eyes, trying to forget the possibility of being seen. Witness. That idea that shot through him in flaccid waves of anxiety.

He closed his eyes, Jason, and she clamped down, a sudden strong grip that sent pain racking through his testicles and gut. She stepped back as she did it, shoved hard off his shoulder with the hand that had held his hip. He fell, angled forward to the sidewalk, elbow catching first, headphones rattling, Selmer pinging cement.

He sat up—it was almost immediate, but it felt like waking—and craned around to watch Lizbeth Princess running out of the Circle, across the roundabout. She ran gracefully—the bar joke used to be a Heisman trophy in pink—dodging a black Mercedes with diplomat plates. From there on, he could see her only through the passing cars, as she pulled the money from his can and threw the can unceremoniously down the steps of a Metro.

Unrealizable thoughts chastened him. *Catch her. Chase her. Call the police.* Of course, there wasn't anyone there, except the old men playing clock chess, unseeing in their focus, indifferent to anything as incomprehensible as bodies that moved of their own volition.

His left elbow was ashen, bleeding in gobs from the sieve of his skin. Jason. His left hip ached. A small dent tarnished the side of his bell. To his ear, it didn't affect sound, but he'd never stop seeing it as damage.

His can wasn't in the Metro when he got there. It took him longer to find a replacement than he'd hoped. Unlike New York, the dumpsters and trash bins in the District tended to be hidden, locked in the alley backyards of homes and businesses, especially those with large items: cracked five gallon buckets, cardboard boxes, industrial-sized cans of succotash, peas.

When he'd started playing the street, he hadn't bothered with questions like these. He was busy convincing himself the fact of it wasn't an embarrassment, busking was a tradition of harmonic adventurers: Bird, Moondog, Sonny Stitt. But the iconic image of the streetcorner sax man with his case full of dollars and change turned out to be impractical.

Nervous listeners would stand at a distance, throw their pocket's worth of dimes in his direction. He would have to pick them up while he remembered where they'd landed, or accept half were lost in cement cracks, drainage vents, patches of grass.

The searching made him seem like a beggar, and the hard flung coins, worse, would sometimes hit reeds, crack them inside their paper sleeves. It could cost more in subway tokens than you made for it.

Bills would blow on a light breeze. He'd have to chase them, or else watch somebody steal his take. A certain sort could ignore you, move on, not looking back. Most couldn't help but meet your gaze—still had the gall to walk off with your money—their shoes tamping guilt into the sidewalk.

He'd almost worked up the nerve once to tell a guy off. It was back in New York, during his first days on the street. He was standing near a corner, outside a pub in Lower Manhattan, late in the day, the sidewalk almost empty: just a couple women chatting a block and a half down, some dingy-looking cat bumming around an empty bagel shop, two dudes in Brooks Brothers, young and lean, their fitted-suit strides marching towards him. The taller of the two, a black-haired guy with bright eyes, had pulled his wallet out as they approached. The shorter one, a stub-nosed blond, said something like, "You're not going to give this guy money, are you?"

"He's good," the tall man said. "It's a tough business."

"He's begging," said the blond, and while the tall man squatted to lay a dollar in his case, the blond faced up to Jason, unfazed by the volume of the horn.

"Hey you," he said. "You think I can get some money? I'm here with you. You want to give me some money? You play, I dance. We're both artists." He kicked heels back in mock tap shoe. "Gotta support each other, right?" They were near enough now Jason could smell the sharp, sweet scent of cologne and liquor sweat and what he imagined was expensive scotch. He kept running the changes to "I Remember Clifford," crescendo, crescendo, while the blond backed away in a drunkard's sort of two-step, tie trailing toes across his zipper. "Buy me a beer, huh?"

The tall man pulled a five from his wallet, added it to the take before standing. "Don't be an asshole," he said.

"Fuck," said the blond, dismissed him with a flick of the wrist and a sideways crisscross up the sidewalk.

Jason ended his solo with a Lee Morgan quote he'd been tooling around with, and it was about then, returning to the head, that the wind caught a crumpled one, carried it tumbleweeding in the men's direction—money drawn to them, he still thinks that. The blond saw it, turning side over side, bent down to pick it up, as it passed. He angled around, holding the dollar to the air by a corner, as if to call a cab, his scarf waving parallel the bill beneath his arm. "That wasn't even the good stuff," he shouted. "What'll you give me for a lap dance?"

The tall man looked to Jason with a useless shrug, and Jason found himself walking towards them then, though they were turned around, already heading Uptown.

"Hey," he called, unhooking his horn. That was as far as he got, just several steps and that *Hey*, and they were gone, around the corner, on their way to well-paying jobs, or by that time, away from them—to families, to bars, to dinners, to homes. You never really know. You imagine it as what you imagine you can't have.

That's the real apology, isn't it: I didn't see you 'cause you didn't see me—and I don't know who started it. Lord knows, it's an egg before the chicken, but at some point you can't tell who the chicken really was. Though you're sure as shit clucking 'round the yard.

Jason turned around, a dollar short, pissed. He hated that kind of shit, because even—perhaps especially—when he was playing out, he'd considered the whole thing, the street, both a way to share his gifts and a kind of business. He believed—still believes—making music, really making music, whatever the circumstances, is the hardest thing a person can do. It requires more than talent. It necessitates practice, skill, concentration. Jazz is like Buddhism. It's about knowing the structure you live inside in order to move out. The more you know the harder that gets.

On top, you got to pay your bills—like everybody else. That's structure number one.

And here some self-righteous prick comes in and busts up his vibe. It's hard to play after a thing like that. He could put up with a lot, but that was the sort of thing that created anger, the kind of anger that entered your mind and couldn't make it past your fingers, your tongue. It was a cold day. His fingers ached. He'd have killed to go inside. That's still how he remembers it, what it means in his mind.

A man was standing by his case, homeless or poorly shaven. He had on an old Fleetwood Mac T, torn under the armpits. "I kept an eye on your stuff," the man said.

"Thank you," Jason said, and sat down against the side wall of the pub. He set his Selmer on the sidewalk beside him, pushed the case lid shut. Just that gust of the lid had enough shove to move bills. The five wafted part way out, one corner in the seam bent slightly towards the ground. He laid his head on his knees, his hands on his head, covering ears and releasing them in measured patterns against bus breaks and the odd metal sounds of the city.

"Yeah, man. I didn't want nobody stealing it."

Jason gave up the pattern. "That's kind, man," he said, and the man stepped closer, shadowed him from the setting sun. "I appreciate it, man. I do," he said. "I don't mean to be a dick. But, can I get a minute?"

"Man, yeah. I protected your shit," the man said. "Kept nobody from stealing it."

"I know, man." Jason craned his neck up, tried to meet his eyes. "Listen, I'm grateful, but I really don't want to talk right now."

"I mean you ran after that dude. Just anybody could've walked up in here and emptied you out." The man's hands flailed with a dubious wonder.

"Yeah, I know, guy. It was stupid. I lost my cool."

"Anybody," the man went on, those hands flapping manically, "could have just come up in here and took all your shit."

Jason came to all fours, stood. "Yeah," he said. "Thanks." He leaned over, picked up his sax, put the reed in one cheek, began to take apart his horn. "Thanks a lot, but, uh, this reed here's on its last legs. I'm going to have to get another box before the shop closes."

"Give me five dollars," the man said.

Jason squatted and turned his case in towards himself. He tucked the five in, laid his Selmer atop the bills and loose change.

It bothered him—still does—to think of coins scraping his bell. He imagined scratches in the brass, heard a grating metallic swish that ached his ears. The mindless action of anxiety: need that is being no one in particular at all. Hands quivering you. The reed went in its sleeve, mouthpiece, neck into baize. Jason closed the case, carried it to his blankets and backpack.

"I protected your shit."

"I know." He slung the backpack over his arms, exhaled under the weight—he carried so much then— bent down, back turned, to gather bedsheets. "I appreciate it."

"Hey, fuck you, man," the man said. "Anybody could have come in here and taken your shit. You can't spare five bucks for the man that kept that from happening."

"I don't have five bucks."

"I saw your fucking case," said the man. "I protected your fucking money." Somewhere in the near distance a truck was backing up, a steady, alerting beep.

"Yeah, man, I know," said Jason. "It's all I got. This is how I make mine."

They were standing close now, this man was standing close. Jason looked at him square on for the first time, into jaundiced eyes. Took in his smell: cigarettes and vinegar and sweat. His own smell, Jason.

The truck still backing up. "You wouldn't have any money if I didn't take care of it, now would you?"

"There isn't anybody here."

"I know, man, I made sure of that."

"Don't do this to me."

"I aint doing this to you," the man said and butted the front of his boot sole into the front of Jason's sneaker.

Jason set his case down, got on knees to open it. He took two ones from inside. "Couple?"

"Five," the man said.

Jason pocketed the ones and pulled the five from under his horn. He handed it to the man.

"You know, man. You sound real nice. Not some of these dudes, coming out here, playing bullshit," the man said. "No, man, you sound real nice. I like that. You're a real player."

By the time Jason had found an old shaving cream box behind a CVS, the sun was near down, painted lines over the Capitol. He was drenched in sweat but his mouth was dry, couldn't wet a reed to get a clean sound. He could smell himself, spiced, putrid. The sidewalks where he was weren't well-used, and the rush and dinner hours were almost over.

Might not have been so bad, but he felt it. No money, not even bus fare, he started the walk to the hostel, where he arrived around the time the street lamps stirred on.

He didn't have rent, and the hippie manager let him stay in an unused bed. He tried to thank her with a kiss she wouldn't allow him, not even after he'd showered. Just said, "You got a tear in your shoe, babe," went up to her own room to sleep.

What can you say of this feeling: anger that's righteous and does you no good, that drives plots of revenge into your mind that could only play out in Warner Bros. cartoons and Wodehouse novels, even there, are disastrous to their plotters. Wile E. Jason Coyote. Those first two days after meeting Lizbeth Princess, he thought of little else but how the thing had happened, how he could right it. Get him some skates and Acme anvils.

The midweek he spent playing Coltrane fake-ups. Not Coltrane—not dignified. Not even Ornette Coleman or Pharoah Sanders. He made noise those days without regard to timbre or sense. In the hottest parts of the afternoons, he would head down to the bars in Adams Morgan, ask if anyone knew a queen, Elizabeth, Liz, Beth something or other, who he'd seen perform and hoped to get for an AIDS benefit. They either looked at him as if he were absurd, or as if he were dangerous, or pointed him to the Madam's Organ, said she did a Thursday night blues cabaret.

Adams Morgan was no place to be in the daytime. It wasn't dangerous, it was a bar district, empty. After a while, he'd head back towards the Capitol, squawk more noise for the day's rent, and the city.

On Thursday, he spent the afternoon on love tunes by the zoo. Between "There Will Never Be Another You" and "A Kiss to Build a Dream On" he would sit on a Bb blues for an entire half hour. Couldn't handle anything more complex. His mind was gone, beyond him, beyond thought, like a million quarters scraping brass inside his ear canal.

At three o'clock, he wandered down to the panda cages. He'd never seen them, never been to a zoo really, except in St. Louis, once or twice, as a child. That one flickered in his mind as an oval track with an aviary of landscaped vines and welding.

There was an Italian ice stand by the Asian Trail. A couple kids came running away from it, cups in one hand, tongue depressors in the other. Jason stopped, let them split him like a pole. When they passed and he was walking again, the sole of his sneaker gave out. The hole, that had only been a hole, had extended to an arc, and that one small stop was the step that did it, the act that changed the facts and definition. Friend of Bill's once asked, *If there's even two bottles, the bottom of what? You gotta want to live.*

That was a thing the street gave him. You go looking for meaning and forget the attention it takes to keep cracked glass from collapsing. You almost don't notice what that does—you know, the good things it does, Jason—for your mind when it's over.

With each step now, the sole flapped back and struck him on the heel with a soft rubber clap. It was funny at first. In his mind, he walked to Cherokee, half-time, Clifford Brown time. 86 beats. Heel claps on the ands of twos and fours. But he was working the sole and the sole was coming further loose, faster for the clapping and the way he sped pace to keep time as the sole fell longer.

It was one of those problems he was too far in to care for. You know the consequences are there, you're paying attention to the consequences, but, at the time, that's the time you're not looking for meaning.

The panda—it was just the one in the heat of the day, the other hiding somewhere cooler—was wavering between bamboo leaves and shade. It came towards the viewing glass, foreshoulders rolling, then sat to eat, lean, lean further into bamboo. Jason knew, without thinking, it was finding a temperature it liked, just right. Goldilocks, this bear in black and white. The small crowd around him giggled and smiled and helloed. A single man in a black tank top pressed his meaty hands to the glass and cooed, "Peekaboo. Peek-a-boo."

Jason left the bear, headed back to Connecticut Avenue, case tapping his thigh, soft slaps of rubber sounding from a foot.

It was amateur night at the Madam's Organ. Despite Pride Week, Jason recalls the bar being oddly barren. Two couples, straight, drinking cocktails at the barfront. Three men, on the bar's far side, wearing three-piece suits and pulling whiskey straight from a bottle they set, between sips, beside a teddy bear with a cigarette-burn belly button. They laughed perpetually, at what, he couldn't imagine, standing as he was outside the door behind a couple getting IDs checked.

The bouncer was unconvinced by the small, thick-cheeked woman in front of him, leaning with feigned exhaustion against the wall.

"What's your birthday?" he asked, looking up briefly, then back at the card.

"May 18, 1969." Something like that.

"Address?"

"1600 Pennsylvania Avenue." She smiled slyly, winked.

"Not funny," said the bouncer. There was plenty of daylight left but his flashlight scanned back and forth across the license, as if he were likely to find something —a smudge of changed ink, poor lamination.

Her girlfriend looked down at her, eyes pushing out in annoyance. The woman just leaned her head to the side so her ear rested in the tall girl's armpit.

"I don't know you need to come in tonight." The bartender offered her card.

"Ramya," the tall girl scolded.

"Erin," Ramya said, wrinkling her nose up to speak in a mocking, nasal whine. She was carrying a fat leather purse on the side of herself closest Erin. She pulled it around her front and began digging. "Here," she said, "my passport."

The bouncer fingered its pages, debating, Jason guessed, whether pride or honest practice was more important. After a minute, he said, "Alright. Come in then." He stepped away from the door, handing Ramya her passport, bowing deeply at the waist as she took it, strutting in.

The bouncer straightened, smiling widely at his cleverness. Jason passed him his driver's license, still from Iowa.

My name is Jason. Hi Jason. Jason Stitch.

"Yeah." The bouncer said, hardly checking. "I don't know you need to come in, buddy." He looked to Jason's feet, tugged at his bottom lip with thumb and forefinger.

"Is it the shoes?" Jason asked. "I can change the shoes. I know it looks dumb, but it happened. I live across town. It's not like I walk around packing spares."

"Yeah. No. I think it might just be better if you went home and stayed there, pal."

"Excuse me."

"I think you've had enough. I'm being good to you now. Head home."

"Had enough?" Jason shouted. He knew it, could feel the stares from the small line behind him, from the people forming queues at bars across the street. "I haven't had a drink in a week. I've had a rough day. My shoe broke walking here. I just want to have a beer and relax."

The bouncer stared hard at the split shoe Jason was holding in the air, flamingo-legged, in evidence of his sobriety, his sober man's sense of balance. He handed Jason the license back, warned him not to make trouble and moved on to the two men behind him.

Jason asked the bartender for something to hold the shoe together. She was a pixieish girl with short hair and sleeve tattoos, the indifferent kind of bartender who'd neither be surprised nor bothered. She asked no questions and gave him masking tape she found in a drawer, popped the Rolling Rock he ordered while he forced popcorn into a little waxed bag.

He taped the shoe at a long angle, heel to string. Tested the job he'd done, walking to the bathroom, and the cheap tape came loose at first step, not failing exactly but adding arrhythmic paper sounds to his movements.

He sat back down at a table against a far wall, sipped the beer and filled his mouth with thickly-greased popcorn he shook from the bag into a palm. He drank and watched large women with ice cream swirl hairdos sweep in and disappear behind the heavy velvet curtains of the stage.

He was on his second—it must have been his second, for years it was his second, D.C. to two months ago, his second—when Lizbeth Princess stepped out from behind the velvet. She swung the curtains open with an arm extended. The backstage briefly exposed, queens behind her tittered with irritation. Lizbeth was wearing blue jeans and a tight camisole that exaggerated the bob of her breasts as she marched—not towards him exactly. She looked beyond to a lower floor stairwell. To the basement, to an exit?

"Hey," he called.

"Hi," Lizbeth answered and walked past with a practiced, unconnecting smile.

He turned his chair, tracking her direction. His forearm caught the beer, and the bottle hit the table top, spurting whitish foam. He righted it, and by then, Lizbeth was gone, down already wherever the steps led.

He almost left, convinced she'd run, escaped. Escaped from what, Jason? He couldn't accept that she'd ignored him. That he meant nothing, not even as a mark. If he'd scared her—he hadn't thought of it as scaring—she'd been caught. Then she'd escaped. He drank on it, brooded. Though Lizbeth did come back. Up the steps, right past him, with the same blank smile while he drank a second.

"Excuse me," he said, "Excuse me," in crescendoing tones. But she strutted backstage like he wasn't speaking at all.

He spent an hour, two beers, watching the curtain's gap. Padded bras were donned. Faces shaved and caked with makeup to smooth skin and erase small hints of stubble. Then she appeared. The real Lizbeth Princess, witnessed for the first time in full regalia, was gorgeous, standing in front of the burgundy curtains in a black dress and patent black pumps. She was hurrying through the room, trying not to be seen.

"Excuse me," Jason slurred. "Remember me?" He took a swig of his beer, a dumb attempt to seem assertive, calm, but he knew he was stiff, ridiculous. He knew that she knew. He kept eyeing her, even as he drank, so hardly any beer made his mouth from the near-empty bottle, a horizon.

"Can you wait a minute, honey." Lizbeth tilted her head towards the bathrooms. Her skin shown darker than he remembered. Her hands were smaller.

"You don't remember me from DuPont Circle? Asking me to go to your car?"

Lizbeth was wearing Coke bottle frames, à la Monk or Buddy Holly. She took them off with one hand, put a fist to her hip with the other. "Listen, baby," she said, pointing a derisive finger. "I know what I must look like to you at one of these shows. But I do this because I'm proud of who I am. And *I am not* some cheap whore you can just walk in here and pick up."

"I don't need your bullshit." Jason said.

"You don't need my bullshit?"

"Listen," he insisted. Listen, Jason, listen. "I could give two shits about your dress code. But I was being nice. It's fucked up that you took my bucket. That was everything I made—"

He knows the rant went on. Listen. Listen. I'm Jason. Hi Jason. He knows it. He told her every awful thing he ever thought of, and instead of shouting back, she just softened with the tempo as his voice ran itself down.

There she was, Lizbeth Princess, with her matte-rouge lips and her eyes shadowed blue, half laughing in bemusement. She laid the Monk glasses on the table, took the thin straps of her dress, pulled them down over her arms, one at a time. She took the top of the dress at the line of her cleavage, slid her thumbs slowly down towards her navel, an outie.

By the tips of her fingers, she raised her skirt, Marilyn Monroe giving in. That's how he tells it. There was a glimpse of a thigh, slightly stretchmarked. Silk drawers falling to the straps of her heels. She lifted one foot out of her panties and drew the second leg up in a tree pose to take the panties in hand without bending.

"This shit happens every couple months, honey. Some motherfucker with my face claiming to be me. I live my life as a woman.

"Did this fellow who robbed you have these?" Lizbeth held her breasts. They rippled near the armpits as she shook them. "He have an ass like this?" She turned a hip to Jason's table, took the dress in both hands, drew it up. She let the skirt fall and pulled her far leg around to square herself to him. "You get back to his car and see this much?" Tucking her skirt under her elbows, she used both index fingers to split the sides of her labia, small and rich purple in the bar light. A holler came from behind him, an enthusiastic *whoo* from Ramya.

"Oh god," Jason said.

"Honey, it's not your fault."

"No," he said. "I'm sorry. I just—she looked like you."

"Honey, you aren't the first. I told you." She said, "Happens every couple months." Jason laid his arms on the table, elbows in popcorn husks and spilled lager. He laid his head on his arms and laughed, and she hugged him then, Lizbeth Princess. He felt her hands pull him gently in and her still naked chest laying sweetly against his forearm, a volley of hollering from the bar.

Of all the things that happened in that two years away from home, this is what is certain: the lips of Lizbeth Princess pressed against his temple, how she held him close and told him it would be alright. How he believed her. How he knew somehow that she knew. How he laughed, how he laughs at all the rest he doesn't know.

A PROBABLE HYPOTHESIS

...We assessed regional and demographic data in pertinent districts, including in Wisconsin—which is what surprised us—Iowa, Pennsylvania, and Ohio. The modeling we conducted considered newly redistricted areas before and after map changes, as awareness on the part of residents that they belong to a particular voting block does *significantly* alter the behavior of undecideds. With less than a five percent margin of error, we determined that one hundred million in advertising spread across the four electoral regions in question would "guarantee" (.912) the Senator a nearly twenty percent lead in the polls. Thus, we recommended you spend accordingly, primarily on "attack ads"—yes—because, at this point in the process, developing name recognition was a useless endeavor, as, with some qualifications, would have been appealing to the Senator's evident stances and well-publicized accomplishments.

We believe Mrs. Baylor's campaign was statistically unpredictable in much the same way one-hundred-year rains are. That is to say, while we could have accounted for the variable of *a* Mrs. Baylor—she did, we admit, petition to be on the ballot—her lack of campaigning prior to the last two weeks of the election cycle led us to dismiss her, along with several others, as "registered" but "inactive." The rain is one in one hundred, as an approximate average. The best one can do in defense against it is to maintain a well-sealed house as a place to weather the storm. Moreover, if you will allow the continuation of the metaphor, one does not accuse the builder of such a house if the wind sends a branch through one's window and one finds one's carpets wet.

Of course, we recognize there is no replacing some things. Yes, this is an "unfortunate setback" for the Senator, and, yes, if you "can still trust us at all" you are correct in your assessment that he is unlikely to retake the Party's vote or the seat he has abdicated. Let us remind you we most certainly did *not* recommend he so brazenly state: "I will always provide for the people of Florida. Right now, I'm doing that by leaving you in the hands of one of the best men I know. Right now, I'm doing that by heading to the White House...." so on and so forth. We "predicted," as you say, and we maintain, that in all likelihood (.893) the Senator would have lost his seat due to the previous June's redistricting and consequent voter attrition in districts critical to his margins. He, and not we, chose to avoid this probable embarrassment with pomp and dramatics. If you are displeased with the results, we recommend you confront the Senator's communications team.

But to answer your most pertinent inquiry, we simply cannot develop a tool for explaining how this "little old biddy" made so many pies in a fortnight, nor so many of the right kinds of friends....

GRACIE'S STORY

My mother would have said that the domestic dispute Dave and I had was *pretty tacky*. She would have said it was really *white trash*. Which Dave's mother says is pretty white trash of her, while Dave's mother makes air quotes with her fingers. I do not know if our domestic dispute was tacky, but I do know that many are more dramatic.

If we lived in a glass house, I would not have hit Dave in the face. Not because the neighbors would have seen. We never have cared much about the neighbors. And we are not pretty enough for them to worry much about. I bet even our sex life would look pretty boring to them—not that there is much of it, or that it lasts long when there is.

The thing of it is this: that I hit Dave in the face, not with my fist, not even with a good bitchslap. It was more like what my mother would have called a *sissy swing*. When I hit Dave in the face, my fist was half-closed, and I got him with the knuckles near my fingernails.

If we lived in a glass house, I would have thrown Dave through a window, which I guess, in that case, would also have been a wall. And then, when the neighbors all looked out from behind their Walmart curtains, the mess would have been impressive.

I do not know exactly how I would have thrown Dave out of the window-slash-wall. He is six-foot-six and has a beer belly, though he doesn't drink any beer at all. I am five-foot-three, which is something that makes us an interesting couple, apart from our domestic dispute.

If we lived in a glass house with window-slash-walls, that would also be an interesting thing about us, but we live in a brick apartment with drywall-walls that are off-white, like the color of factory-farm eggs. Even if I were six-foot-six and the fit kind of woman that people would watch have sex through her glass window-slash-walls, I probably could not throw Dave through our drywall-walls, nor would I want to.

I do not want to hurt Dave because I think that I love him.

I say I think because I have never been in love before. I have also never lived with a man before, or with anyone except for my mother, who is gone. I have never lived with a man before, or hit him. Dave deserved it though, or at least I thought so at the time. But this incident might have gotten out of hand.

Dave didn't call the cops. I did. Dave had been playing his French horn, and it was bothering the neighbors. They don't pay much attention to us, but they do knock on their side of the drywall when Dave plays his French horn after it is dark. Dave is in the symphonic band at the community college and is the first chair in the French horn section, which Dave is proud of, even though most of the French horn parts for the symphonic band at the community college are unison and just to add what Mr. Hawkins calls *color*. I know this because I am the second chair French horn and because our parts only have "French horn" written on the top left corner of the first page, and all our notes are the same.

I do not practice with Dave, though, after it is dark, because I work third shift at the cheese plant, in Monroe, which means that I clean the machines and toilets. It might sound gross, but I like the toilets better. Dave says that I am a janitor, but I like to think that I am more than that. Dave is a mechanic, who works on diesel engines, and that is pretty good.

Dave says I am pretty good at the French horn, which was sweet, when he was trying to get a date with me. But now it is not. Now, I want him to know that I am better at the French horn than he is. Which I am.

Mr. Hawkins, who directs the symphonic band at the community college, told me I was the best French horn player he has ever had. I am not sure how long that ever is, but Dave was already there when I joined the band, which is why he is the first chair and is how I met him.

I hit Dave because he got mad at me. He was playing his French horn, and it was late, too late for practicing. I know, because the neighbors were knocking. I told him that, and he got mad at me. I am not sure why. The neighbors were knocking on their side of the drywall-walls. Maybe he hadn't heard them because he was playing so loud.

If we lived in a glass house, I would not have to tell Dave when the neighbors are knocking. He would see them through the glass window-slash-walls looking very unhappy. Dave is like me, though, and doesn't always know what people mean to say with their faces. So maybe, Dave would have kept playing—which is why I had to hit him. That and the fact that I am a better French horn player than he is, and because he doesn't know it.

I called the cops because this is how you have a domestic dispute: you have an argument with your boyfriend, and you hit him or, more usually, he hits you. Then the cops get called, and if it is interesting enough the cops will send the film of your domestic dispute to a TV show on Fox Television, where you will appear with your faces pixelated.

Our faces will not be pixelated on Fox Television. But the neighbors did look at us when the cops came and talked to us. We have four neighbors at our apartment, two in each apartment on either side. But there are forty-three people in the complex where we live, and because many of their apartments face our apartment, many of them looked out from behind their curtains to see our domestic dispute.

Dave was still crying when the cops came, and I felt sorry that I had made him cry. I tried to tell Dave I was sorry about hitting him. But I don't think he heard because the crying was so loud, and because the neighbors were still knocking.

The first time I kissed Dave after band practice, he cried then also. His tears fell into a puddle lit by the moon and the lights of the community college parking lot, white and yellow and white. This made the puddle look sharp, as if there was a piece of glass in it. Or maybe there was a piece of glass in it. I didn't stop to look because Dave was bawling. When his mother saw this, she came out of the van and got Dave, and she laughed the whole while.

While I was worried Dave's mother would be mad at me about our domestic dispute, she was not all that mad. Dave told the cops he did not want me to go to prison. The cops called Dave's mother, who came and got him. Before she left, I said to her that I was sorry. She said that she thanked me for my apology, and told me all couples have bumps in the road. Because of the way we are, Dave and I have a few more bumps than others. But I think I love Dave, and I think Dave loves me, and we are trying.

Dave's mother says she will probably bring him home tomorrow. I do not get lonely really, but I have gotten used to having Dave in our apartment. I will feel happy when Dave comes home tomorrow. Because I think that I miss him.

AND GOOD WILL TOWARDS MEN

Peace the bear asks Donkey, "What's happening?"

"A baby," Donkey says. "Mary and Joseph are having a baby." Janet picks him up and neighs. She knows that's not what he'd sound like, but hee-haw irritates her and horse seems close enough.

"Janet," says Dad. "Stop that. You're going to break the porcelain." He's rushing through the living room, past the manger, hands filled with rolls of lights. "Mom's going to be back with Joe soon. Give me a hand, why don't you?"

"What do you want?" Janet asks. She leans Peace against the dresser and gets to her feet.

"Oh, I don't know," Dad says. "Bring the wrapping paper up from the basement." And he's gone into the den to string lights up on the tree.

Janet would rather the tree be real, but it's the same old one they always put up, dark and short and smells like plastic. Last year, Mom promised Janet a real tree, a blue spruce, but since then, Joe spent four months in Spain and Dad stopped sleeping in the guest room. Times have changed. And not for the better.

The wrapping paper container is at the bottom of the stairs. And there are two totes too. Two totes full of ornaments and tinsel. They smell like trees—not plastic, but sort of real—because last Christmas, Joe came home and covered the tree with air fresheners, the pine-shaped kind they make for cars. It was a joke, Joe said, about our artificial reality. Mom didn't get it, and neither did Janet. Dad said he read somewhere that air fresheners keep mice out of closets, and threw them in with the rest of the decorations when he took everything downstairs.

Janet opens up the top tote and takes two tree fresheners, strings them from her ears as rings. She picks up the paper container, carries it on her shoulder up the stairs.

Dad's up there. "Having fun?" he asks.

"Yes," says Janet and hands Dad the container.

Joseph hasn't said much. And that's okay. Rachel's glad to have him home—she is his mother—but it's been more peaceful with him abroad, at school. Janet's a more self sufficient child. You wouldn't think it, listening to Joe, with all his talk of liberation and experience, his expostulations on politics, his raw smugness.

Truth told, though—and she is trying, now, to tell herself truths—her son needs people. Wherever he goes, he makes it his first priority to find folks he can attach himself to, whom he can convince he is essential, so he can sit in their passenger seats, watching snow drifts rise as outcroppings in empty fields of corn, imposing on them omens of geography he thinks they cannot understand.

Now that he's home, Joe only talks about Spain, and himself. It was fun when he came in yesterday, carrying his bags full of presents, and said, "Bon festes." But since then he's bon fested everyone he's seen: Grandma (on the phone), the skinny waiter at the breakfast place, twice Janet, and once the cashier at the grocery store. It's like, if he didn't tell everyone about it, he wouldn't have been there. Like if he hadn't been there, it wouldn't be okay.

He's trying to make the whole world Barcelona, Spain. Yesterday, before Janet went to bed, he pulled this stocky log from his duffel and yelled, "¡Caga Tió!" like everyone should know what that was.

Caga Tió is a foot long and has a little dowel nose, with a red tip like Rudolph and two stick legs. It's got a bright face on, smiling Mickey-Mouse-style, a squishy half-moon with a big tongue and line-drawn cheeks, and no teeth at all. "Tió de Nadal," Joe said. "The Christmas Log." He said, "The Shitting Log," bitterly.

The log's sitting in the den now, beneath Dad's tree. It's only four in the afternoon, but the sun is coming down. The den is on the house's east side. The lights from the tree are beautiful, yellow-white and gleaming like little suns, like each one is The Star and she should follow it. But that log is sitting there beneath. Caga Tió, watching her.

Whether she's in the living room or the dining room, it can see her. It is wearing its little red hat and watching her with its constipation. Janet stays in the kitchen. She asks Mom if she can help bake cookies.

Rachel is trying to be practical. John's parked on Pitchersville Street, near enough it's plausible she's only taking a walk. He's idling in front of the Califf house, the motor of his Chevy purring laboriously, exhaust rising white and bilious across the rear windshield. Today, his text messages have said simple, pleading things: *I miss you… I love you… Meet me. Please!!!! Just to talk…*

The last few weeks he's stopped sending messages about his cock—how much he wants her to suck it, how much he misses her, how much he enjoyed her sucking it, how Jacob wouldn't know if she sucked it, just one more time, one more time, just one more time. A month or so after she agreed to end this, she had, and while she's thought a lot recently about taking up with someone again—not John, but someone with whom she could have fun, be responsible—she hasn't. Her marriage: she knew it was gone long before John— needy fool—and Jacob must have known this too. Joe certainly did. But Janet can still have a life like Rachel always imagined. She can be close to somebody. She can be happy.

The passenger side door of the Cavalier is locked. Rachel wipes its window with her mitten. John, from inside, can be seen doing the same, his ruddy face particulating with each wave of their hands around a slowly melting circle. He is smiling cherubically, tobacco-stained teeth gleaming off-white beneath the overhead lamp. She crosses her arms, holding her biceps. She turns her torso from side to side in mock drama of the chill. He pulls the door handle, and she waits for him to erect himself in the driver's seat so she doesn't have to touch him.

"You came," he says, as if surprised. As if she'd often left him waiting in the cold. It isn't true—not with John.

She never lied.

"I came," she says. Sitting down, she buckles herself in, pulls her coat close to her chest, warms her neck with fisted mittens. "How've you been?"

"You know me." He turns on the engine as if to defy her need for brevity. "Same old."

After Mom left, Joe brought Caga Tío into the living room and sat him next to the bureau. It was too much. Janet worked up her courage to turn him around, so he was facing the wall. Now Dad is sitting on the loveseat next to Janet. They are watching *The Island of Misfit Toys*.

Since he quit his job at the cheese plant, Dad's started to talk a lot about the environment. He's taking classes in Rockford to be a DNR officer. He keeps telling Mom that his friends—Bob and Gene and Richard, the ones he goes fishing with—tease him about cutting them slack, "which is the same," Dad's explained, "as saying they expect you to be an asshole." Dad is threading popcorn on a string. Janet is eating it straight from the bowl. Dad says the birds can eat it too, if he winds the string around the jack pine in the yard. "We can pull the string down after the holidays. We won't have wasted any electricity."

Janet asks if they can talk about it during the commercial break. The Toy Taker is taking the Misfit Toys, like he took Santa's before, and Queen Camilla's. He is playing his flute, the Toy Taker, to lead the toys to his giant vacuum, not even noticing Rudolph, Hermey, Clarice, some others from their gang are hiding in the line. They are waiting to rescue the toys who've been vacuumed up, to save Christmas!

"And it's not like rice at weddings," Dad says, ignoring her. "Already popped. It won't swell in their stomachs."

"What?" Janet asks. The Abominable Snow Monster, Bumble, is wearing a pink rabbit costume. It's a good disguise, but he's too big to be sucked into the Toy Taker's ship. He wants to help his friends but can't. Big Bumble Rabbit is crying.

"The popcorn," Dad says. "It's already popped. It won't grow in the birds' stomachs. It won't hurt the birds."

"Oh," Janet says. "That's good." The Toy Taker apologizes for not being able to carry Bumble away.

Joe comes from his room. He is putting on his coat. But nobody wants to talk to Joe. So, for a second, nobody talks, and Janet is given a break from listening to Dad, from everything but the show. "I'm heading out," says Joe, "into the frigid night."

"Have fun," says Dad. He threads three more kernels onto his string.

Joe walks a few laps between the bureau and television. "I'm ill-equipped," he says on the umpteenth turn. "The Mediterranean weather's spoiled me. I'm no good now in the freeze."

"Shut up," says Janet. She knows he's joking, but it still annoys her.

"Probably die of exposure."

"Probably," Dad says. Janet turns the volume up so high her eardrums crackle. Dad tells her to knock it off and takes the remote from her hand.

Joe is petting the manger, where it sits now, on the bureau top. It looks ragged, musty. The wood is dark and seems to be molding, though it's really very clean— two-years old and covered in paint and stain and dyed-cotton moss. Mary and Joseph appear to be—are— having their baby in the worst of places. But he is the Savior of the World. Janet's brother, her stupid brother, doesn't get this. He's stroking the moss. Being melo-dro-matic, Mom would say. "I'm going to freeze to death," says Joe.

"You better get started," Dad says. There is a sad song playing on the TV behind a slough of starving animals.

"I'm going to freeze to death sucking dicks in a snowbank."

"God dammit, Joseph," Dad yells. But Joe just topples the manger onto the floor and walks past the couch and goes, half-laughing, out the door.

Dad gets up quickly, knees bent low, nostrils wide, like he means to chase him. But after a minute of standing there, Dad just says, "I'm sorry," and sits back down with his needle pinched between two fingers, leaving every sheep and Magi scattered on the carpet.

It must be said that Mary is unused to being touched, least of all unasked by wooden strangers. She was born in a factory in Northeast Mexico, where she was held and inspected by a single woman, before being placed in her Styrofoam bed.

There she was raised, in purity, prophylactically protected from the sinful-looking men who stacked her family on a pallet and locked them in a truck to be shipped to a warehouse in Rockford, to be again pallet-stacked, then unstacked and stacked and shifted, and shifted and shelved in the Freeport Walmart, where Dad would, for the first time, lift her from her bed and stare admiringly at her sacred blue cloak, unmarred, for all that, by the journey.

Until now, with the reasonable exception of brushes from Joseph's right sleeve and bumps from the head of Donkey—who is a male, too, but a eunuch—Mary has never been touched by any man other than Dad. Adjusted, by women—yes—Grandma and Mom. Rubbed—yes!—lovingly, by a single thumb of Janet's. But this—this!—is unacceptable. Caga Tío, that shit-eating grin on his face, is straddling her, holding her waist with one pine leg, pushing down with his backside, as if to force them both into the carpet.

It's the contrasts she finds most enticing. The way the frigid air weighs in around the car, making her joints stiff and mind lucid. The softness of his body, the heat of his stomach, sweater-warm and beer-fat and covered with rough black hair. The uneven lamplight outside, so broad in the open night, the directness of the nearest light coming in through the little-frosted passenger-side window. The rest is near darkness, the Cavalier made igloo, darkness and knee knocks and harried kneading motions.

Her hands fumble for hips, for a comfortable position, to draw him in. John kisses. He ruts in her neck. He bites.

She says, "Don't bite."

He grunts.

She says, "Quiet."

There is a figure outside, passing toward the Califf's, very tall. She thinks, Dr. Califf, the chiropractor, perhaps snooping on his ex-wife, looking for his key. John is kissing, neck and neck and neck: she thinks if she kissed him this way his head would pop right off. She can barely feel the tip of him, her legs stripped bare, her jeans around an ankle, the inside of her thighs pressed terribly close.

The shadow, his body, awful close. She knows he isn't looking for a key now, whoever he is. He is watching, hands in jacket pockets, arms akimbo, so, in silhouette, he appears as a man with tiny wings, watching as the sweat of John's body frosts the window, again, white.

"Excuse me," Mary says at Caga Tío. "Excuse me."

Peace, who's spent the evening sitting against the dresser, watching the Shitting Log—Janet trusts him to protect the others—gives Mary an unblinking stare.

"This can't be," Mary says, to no one in particular. Then to Dad, "Come pick me up. Why don't you come pick me up?"

"He will," says Peace. Though Peace is worried. The whole Manger family is sprawled across the floor. They all seem to be intact, but Peace thinks the building might be damaged. Dad is doing that thing he does when he is really fighting with Mom, which is to say, Dad is doing exactly the thing he was doing before the argument: threading popcorn on a string with a needle.

"Where's Janet?" asks a Magi lying face down near the table. Even Peace, who is Ty and tie-dye, so many colors—fifteen faded shades of purple, blue, green, pink —can see this king is turning green with the smell of his own gifted incense.

"She is doing what she always does," reports Donkey, who is lying on his side very near Janet's foot, "when Dad is mad." She is doing what she does, which is doing what he does: now, watching a L'oréal commercial, eating popcorn, hardly listening to Dad speak about indigenous, non-migratory birds, while pretending nothing's happened.

"Help!" cries Joseph. "Help, help."

"Oh, Joseph, dear, where are you?"

"Beneath the manger, Mary. Beneath the manger. Help, help."

"Help," cries the Magi tumbled against the sofa.

"Help," bleat the sheep clustered near the chair.

"Help," shouts the owner.

"And help," shouts his wife.

"*Hah-elp!*" bellows Cow, whose whole belly rests on the face of the third Magi, who is mumbling something very much like Help.

"Help!" and "Help!" and "Help!" they yell. But everyone is yelling for himself.

When Rachel returns from her walk, Joseph is sitting on the front steps smoking a black cigarette, reading a novel—she would guess, though the cover is blank and cotton-bound, and when she sits next to him, with her head on his shoulder, peering over at the two open pages, she sees it's in Spanish, or Catalan. Rather than ask, she says, "A little cold out here for that, yeah?"

"Yeah," he says and sets the book down with a far-off brooding that's a little practiced. He turns to her so she has to lift her head, and takes her face in his hands. They're frigid, his hands. They slide down her neck. His fingers, middle and fore, press in and up along her jawline, behind her ears. In the back of her throat, where it meets her sinuses, Rachel feels a gentle, viscous draining. "Not me, Mom. If anyone's going to be sick, it's you." He says, "You're a little flush. Lymph nodes swollen."

"Are you a doctor now?" she asks. She takes his wrists, setting them on his lap, and picks up his book, pretending.

"No," he says, "not yet." He ashes his cigarette. "But I know things."

"I know you know things." She pinches a finger on his opened page. "Spanish."

He adds, "And Catalan," and takes the book back.

"But this is Spanish," she says.

"This *is* Spanish," he says.

"Yes," she says and takes the book back and runs a thumb along a rough and yellowed corner.

"He can be a real ass, you know," says Joe. "Una—"

"You can be a real ass, hombre," she says. He frowns at this and turns from her.

"Do you want to get a drink?" she asks.

The yard looks freshly dusted with newly fallen snow. Though it hasn't snowed, not since late-November. The temperatures fell then—too cold for snow, for melting, too cold to sit outside because it is never too cold for wind. The wind seems not to know they live in the middle of town, where the wind should catch between, be deadened by, squat houses.

Crystal flakes shake from rigid drifts, levitate in swirling turns across the yard and the yards of their neighbors, from which porch lights shine on their yard, which is not porch-lit. The snow in front of their house gleams white with mica glints, when bodies move as shadows.

In the middle, a light from the living room, flashing on and off in reds and blues, the television illuminates the jack pine, which Rachel's husband has strung with popcorn tinsel, which quivers on its thread, wind-tickled and laughing with curious desires.

"Yeah," Joseph says. "Why not?"

Mom and Joe come in together. Janet peers at them over the back of the loveseat. Mom's arm is strung through Joe's. They are laughing. Joe looks at Janet for a second too long, puzzled.

"¡Bon festes!" he shouts.

"Help!" yell all the Mangers. "Help, help."

"Keep it down," barks Dad, baking nutloaf in the kitchen.

"You keep it down," Mom says, also drunk, tongue sloppy-showing while she talks.

Mom and Joe, they are standing in the entryway, waiting for each other to move.

Ralphie's Dad, on the television, gets out of the car. He invites Ralphie to—

"Help!" yells Donkey.

"Déu vos salve Maria, plena de gràcia, el Senyor és amb tu…"

Peace, looking directly at Caga Tío, believes his painted mouth is really moving.

"Hail Mary," says Peace, "full of grace. The Lord is with thee. Blessed art thou among women, and blessed is the fruit of thy womb, Jesus," who, being a child of pride and dignity, speaks in the language of his fatherland, calling from his upturned crib of hay, "Dios te salve, María, llena eres de gracia, el Señor es contigo…"

Rachel closes her eyes. The world has been coming at her, in flashes, one rapid frame at a time.

"Ave-"

"Mary-"

"llena eres de-"

"Help!"

"Shut up!"

"Shut up!"

"You shut-"

"But I didn't say fudge."

Mom doesn't say she is leaving. She just walks off, like a boy you beat in an argument. Through the bathroom wall, you can hear the shower pipes over the sounds of Ralphie's friend being beaten for not saying fudge.

Ten or fifteen minutes later—after Joe's disappeared into his room, after Dad has set an egg timer and vanished into the basement, with the television off and the only sounds in the house the din of water running in the shower and the hush and shush of wind turned wild outside, the incomprehensible chant of these dolls, saying what they are saying in their three doll languages—Janet puts the manger upright, counting each figure as she sets them in their places. "Joseph, one. Donkey, two."

When she is done, she goes to the bathroom. She knocks on the door, softly. Her mother doesn't answer. She opens the door, tiptoes to the toilet, pulls her pants down and her panties. Janet shits, soft and messy from the cookies she's eaten.

In the shower, the water hums still louder, wavering with calcium clogs and an aging pump. The pipes give off a high-pitched whistle. Janet wipes but doesn't flush, it would scald her mother. She doesn't wash her hands, in case the same.

She steps to the shower, takes the blue curtain and pulls it back, pulls back the white sheer curtain also, to find her mother glowing radiant beneath the bright yellow light astride the shower. Down on her knees, her face in her hands, the backs of them resting on the slant of the tub. Her hair is black with wet and clumped in sordid ringlets.

Janet can see what her mother must see, the light and the white tub and the running water, like she was the mountain behind a waterfall. But this only lasts a second. She is not the mountain. Only a girl, eight, nearly nine, her hands dirty, stained mustard-yellow with food coloring and flecks of waste. Janet is the girl called to move the mountain. She steps, in her pajamas, into the shower. She sits behind her mother, legs spread. And takes Rachel by the ribs, holding her upright like the faithful.

THE ELVES AND THE COBBLER

I've taken to sleeping outside, with my body turned out to the alley and the north-facing neighbor's garden. Fall's coming on in Wisconsin. Mornings I wake with dew in my hair, makes me feel leaden all day. I've got a week or two maybe—the news says the ten-day forecast is promising. Maybe we'll skip the first frost and arrive straightaway at Indian summer.

Viktor followed me, once as far as the kitchen window with a homemade beer in his hand. That was the night we'd gone to Gracie and David's and I'd gotten mad and declared to the party that Viktor was a feral child, and everyone except Gracie laughed like I was kidding. *Feral* might not be the term. Viktor knew his father, or he told his doctors so when he finally acquired the gift of gab. After the party we didn't discuss it. I just went and lay down, and he went to staring out the window, looking at me real intently while I tried to see into the neighbors' kitchen, where their cat was entertaining himself with the pullstring on the blinds. I said, "Are you coming?"

He said, "There isn't room."

I said, "You're dumb."

"No, I'm not," he said. "Someone could see us. Someone could walk up the back stairs and stab you if they wanted."

"Who would want to?" I asked.

He got awfully nervous then and took a swig of his beer, full-mouthed, so that foam rose up and dripped onto the tile. "Dammit," he said. "I'm sleeping on the davenport."

This turned out not to be true, or not true all night. In the morning when I came inside, he'd locked himself in the bedroom. Our cat was licking the floor.

This is the problem: that we have begun mimicking each other. That having had expectations of what our otherness might be, we can only see outside ourselves in categories as vast as our ignorance.

Before he moved in in May, Viktor'd never owned a TV. He's been watching Daniel-Day Lewis movies, one per night, because one of his doctors, the first, his friend, this Jean Itard, calls him from France. It's like talking to your mother, he tells me. Some people you know so well, you love with such earnestness, the best you can do is watch the same films alone. He spends all this money on long-distance calls. You have to have something to say.

Gracie's aunt's the same way, I think. She's moved to some mountain town in Italy where she teaches school children to read. Daniel-Day Lewis has a kid in her class. I guess after becoming Cecil Vyse or some oversexed doctor from Prague, he needs time in himself. He lives in Italy, he sleeps with his wife. He cobbles shoes. And I want to give him this time in his cottage and in his industry, same, but—

Someday his wife will wake beside him and say, Let's stay up late to see how, in the night, the leather gets sewn, only to find there are no undressed creatures of the wood, just the tools of her husband, his calloused thumb, the lamp he lights against the darkness. I can't bear this loss of magic. I've no love for all this mystery.

HERITAGE

DRIFTLESS

Years later, I see it, driving through Oklahoma, en route to Arizona. Stroud, OK. Which isn't anywhere and so no different from what've become—Stockton, Illinois, or Elizabeth; or South Wayne, Wisconsin—the places named for their replacements, the women who fended Indians off with muskets, God knows, but of this change. I spoke French two hundred years ago, and the Sauk boys spoke something not French but closer to it than American. The seasons of Mississippi trade holding sounds to the fronts of their mouths.

There are sadnesses for which I am responsible. A Dakota girl sold to an Arkansas trader for a case of whisky darker than her navel. A Chickasaw touched too many times and left swelling when I went West. The tin casino outside Stroud, though. The ceramic buffalo bought with tribal funds, painted white and with meaningless hieroglyphs arrows, teepees, other buffalo painted with buffalo, smaller, smaller.

We were only entertaining the Sauk boys Black Hawk left sitting on the River. Nothing to do all day, just the three of them looking at canoes crossing the east bank. You get so quickly old you forget there are things a boy doesn't know—not to drink with pens or pistols. You never think to tell a lit fellow not to punch the ground. If he does, you wrap his hand, never mention it.

LAW OF CONSERVATION

In the kitchen of the house on Mammoser Road, which her son-in-law bought and in which, for ten years, his own mother lived, looking while she cooked over the sheep grazing the lawn and the hundred-odd acres that were his and, too, the acreage of Joe Mammoser his stepsons split at Joe's passing, that poorer land, her son in-law says, though she doesn't know that it's true, Anna cuts shortening into flour with her mincing knife. Her daughter sifts sugar on rhubarb in a bowl, asks why not a pastry blender. Anna tells her she doesn't own one. Her daughter goes through the drawers, the while explaining, "Not the electric thing"—like Anna doesn't know.

Rita finds it, holds it up. Says, "This, Mom. This."

"I know this." The dough on her cutting board divides in cubes like Turkish delight. She takes her knife's flat edge, levels it haggard, cubes it again. "I don't need this."

"Betsy: your granddaughter." Rita says, "Betsy sent this." Adds, "To help you." She says, "With your baking."

Anna begins folding her dough on itself, rounding it. Too soon: she can see the stains of flour and shortening—skin through a slip. She says, Finished.

"Mom," Rita puts the blender away, "Betsy wants—"

"Rita, Betsy wants recipe cards before I die. Flour: this much. Fat: this much. Delicious."

"Mom," Rita says, and stops.

"This belongs to Suzanne. Karen bought it for Suzanne, not Betsy. She never used it. I never use it. Tell your husband to fix the tractors with it. Tell your daughters to make their own pies with it. The oven lights itself. I have a knife."

POTLUCK

Philippians 2:1-4

Margaret Smith was born in 1927, her daughter Deborah Ann in '43, late July and two days short of her own next birthday. In Stockton, Illinois, this was not a matter of ridicule, neither then nor later, but one for comment, as folks spoke of the fall crop harvest until winter had been so long at its agitations folks began talking of hope by way of planting, standing around the Lutheran Church basement after Sunday potluck, washing community utensils, one old girl in a permanent saying to the next, "That potato casserole was something."

"Yeah, good, huh? Gene, I think she puts more sour cream in than my recipe calls for."

"Is that what it was? Sour cream."

"Yeah. Think so."

"I'll have to try that."

"You see Deb Smith came today? Didn't stay for potluck. Came. Sat in back. Left right after the sermon."

"Yeah, Deb. She's nice, aint she?"

"Real nice. You know her mother had her age of fourteen, fifteen."

"Yeah, think I knew that. She turned out all right. Real nice."

"Real nice. Never comes to potluck."

"Wonder why?"

"Maybe can't cook. Least she don't come and eat everybody else's food. But you're right, I've known her sixty years, and I'd still like to get to know her."

"Yeah. Well. You know, John's been worried it won't thaw soon enough to get the corn planted."

"Oh, it always gets planted. Question's will it grow?"

And, of course, the corn grows, some of it, usually, for most folks who grow it. That year had been cold well into spring and the planting was done later than it should have been, and one day in May—April had been a pride of lions—the air turned into the sixties and stayed there a month straight, so we all got to thinking we were living in some artist's pastoral. Kind of weather you can find something to do in for ten or twelve hours and come home to supper without feeling starved. Kind of weather folks who garden love to garden in—pair of gloves and a sunhat, blue jeans and a nylon blouse. Deb Ann, we'd see her in front of her house when we were driving by the school, and most times her mother too, from sunup to sundown, drinking sun tea and prodding the loam, hunting for sprouts of the weeds they'd already picked.

Deb Ann, folks said, was always a perfectionist. In school, they say, she used to do trigonometry problems in her head, beginning homework with answers she only later filled in the proofs for, working from the last steps so when she arrived again at the questions she seemed always surprised. Many of us born after her would have doubted this, the genius of Deb Ann Smith. She had not, after all, left, as did most minds of the town who showed half so much promise. And she had not taken to teaching, as had the rest. Like her mother her income was unknown, and while neither woman flaunted extravagance, neither did their clothes or their grocery carts show signs of government assistance—little bologna, few potatoes, never used food stamps or ever sold them.

Those two women, who lived together and alone, from the birth of Deborah Ann to Margaret's death on the day of her birthday, 2017, were, without fail, dressed tastefully for whatever tasks they set themselves to while the two of them, like late-age twins, went about the town and garden. Each day they bought effeminate portions of lean meat and greens and bakery rolls, from Sullivan's grocery, no one ever saw them eat.

We speculated on occasion about the Smiths, who were not the Smiths who owned a farm in the middle of Nora. We offered our thoughts on Deb Ann's father: Must've been a soldier. Must've been rich. Deb must be Christ in women's clothing. Might be the father, her father, or some uncle. Why is it anyhow those Smiths north of town are always claiming they're no relation? "All of 'em weird," we'd say, leaving the Lutheran Church basement after Sunday potluck.

"Yeah, well," our husbands would tell us, "aint hurtin' nobody, I guess." Their lack of interest would be the end of it for a while. Months would go by sometimes before Deb Ann came back to church, or 'til we got of mind to talk of her again. Pastor might offer a sermon on community one Sunday—*Do nothing out of selfish ambition or vain conceit. Rather, in humility value others above yourselves, not looking to your own interests but each of you to the interests of the others*—or speak on the indefinable, bodiless qualities of Heaven, and we would be watching our husbands after, plowing through great heaps of oatmeal cookies and mashed potatoes and would declare without apparent connection that we had seen Deb Ann Smith in her garden the other day. Couldn't life be weird.

That she could sit with us and consider the gifts of Jesus and the mystery of Faith and afterwards go immediately home to her mother, who was raised Catholic and had been absent from any church from the first day she showed, that she could go without the sacraments of food and conversation, that she could persist without first letting herself forget—these baffled us. Deb Ann baffled us, and to be so baffled by a woman we were not made the world feel somehow safer. As it did to know our fathers and husbands and grandsons had been to the foreign wars, and that most of them had come back. In a century of wars, we had proven resilient. Nothing terrible came closer than Syria, or New York, or Chicago, or a half-empty bottle thrown at the wall. Single faults and worries, which were in some ways understandable—necessary—like an Amish quilt maker who damages her pattern to leave perfection alone to God.

It was Barb Varner's husband found Peg lying on one side, complaining of chest pains. Deb, I guess, was inside pouring her mother another glass of tea. July then, and muggy hot. Andy Varner claimed her face was so full of dirt and sweat he couldn't tell whether it was her or the daughter when he'd been passing by, on his way to the golf course—this was a year maybe before it closed—his clubs in the back of his pickup. Said he called the fire department shouting, "I'm up here on North Street and Deb Smith is having a heart attack. Peg, I mean. Deb, I mean." The fire department hurried over, and a couple EMTs. It took longer than it ought have: not enough volunteers since the firehouse burned down a couple springs before and the young boys all quit because they had no place to congregate and drink while they told stories. And maybe it would have been too late anyhow, for Peg, old as she was then, 90. But we spoke to each other of the tragedy of it. Said it was a shame. Called down the phone tree, made sure Deb had dinner and a visit every night for a month and a day.

She never welcomed any of us in, never even came to the door, so that we had to stand around knocking and eventually leave our Pyrex dishes on the doorstep with small notes of condolence and our addresses taped to the lids. For hours sometimes, we would drive up and down the block, guaranteeing her food and dinnerware weren't overrun by cats or coons or possums, and if we did that long enough, Deb Ann would appear briefly to collect the food, looking pleased, we supposed, but never thankful, never answering calls after, but leaving our washed dishes as we had, on our doorsteps with brief notes of gratitude. *Dear Mrs. K—, How unimaginably kind. How delicious. Regards, Deborah A. Smith.*

Even Pastor rarely spoke with her, though she answered his calls and his raps at her door. What they talked about he wouldn't say, but he promised us her health and that she was keeping up the household, however we imagined it.

The most of us had been married, and several of those divorced. We had, many of us, had children and loved them through our own faults and confusions, and theirs. When one of the Bentzinger girls brought home a woman, we were perplexed but not dissenting. Pastor, himself, found an officiant for the service, which was held at the church, and well-attended by those who watched the mothers quake with tears. We recognized in ourselves the positions we held, taking of them what we thought considered and best. We believed ourselves forgiving and open-minded, as much as the Unitarians, at least.

I know what other folks say. Exit polls lie, and probably so do the ballot counters. I know too I voted for Hillary Clinton—I didn't especially want to, well, but I did—and she was a woman, and she won. Obama had promised to move Guantanamo to the prison built in the southern part of Carroll County, and he couldn't get it done, like most everything else, because it looked like he was servicing his home state, and laws about this and funds for that, and I thought, Hillary doesn't give a damn about Illinois, and she sure owes Obama. And, well, what were a couple hundred Arabs going to do if they did get out, except run around the bean fields 'til somebody shot 'em.

Guantanamo never got anywhere near here. They did make a show of moving a couple second-rate jihadis to Thomson prison while they waited on trial. And Trump's people sent one scout down to get the lay of the land, the way they did with Obama. Just one old fellow in a black suit and a Cadillac Escalade, asked a lot of stupid questions about how often we looked on our fields and how we thought prison tax revenue would benefit our schools. We weren't even in the same county.

He was around most of that spring, after Donald's inauguration, 'bout eight, nine months after Peg Smith passed—no service, no funeral, not at the Catholic church or ours. He didn't stay in Stockton only, of course, but based out of Thomson and trucked himself through every town as far south as Sebula, north as us, east, we heard, as Elroy. Andy Varner joked if towelheads were so fast they could run from Thomson to Mt. Carroll without being noticed there wouldn't be so many Kenyans winning track gold at the Olympics. Well, Jen Neally, who teaches Western Civics at the high school, protested, but my husband laughed himself so stupid he spit potato salad up on the linoleum, and none of us heard why.

Anyhow, for a while, we thought it was really coming, but the fellow was just shooting bunk to keep the President in the right kind of news.

The government man was gone then for ten or twelve weeks. We didn't see or hear of him 'til about mid-summer, which had gotten awfully muggy awful quick, and stayed that way, so that you hated to be outside for fear of heat stroke and sweat stains showing through your blouse. Deb Smith wasn't even seen in her garden, to speak of, though her tea jar was always on the step next to her door. That's what I picture him by, his Army black shoes grimed with gravel dust and his pant legs pressing against those thighs of his, that hadn't gotten thin like a regular man's, of a certain age, above the flowers of the jar in their monochrome blues, behind the wild prism of flowers hardly tended in Deb Ann's garden. But all we ever saw was the SUV, parked there late at night, or some sturdy man, like he was, passing to that Escalade in the dawnlight.

From time to time, we might see Deb Ann herself, shopping at the store, filling her cart with canned peas and frozen chicken. And we'd say, "Deborah Ann, How you doin', dear?"

She'd say, "Fine. Awfully busy."

We'd say, "Well, I know how that goes. Corn's gettin' tall."

Before the crops came in, before football season, the boys from town treading down her asters as they rushed not to be late for two-a-day practice, before any of us had time to think to say goodbye, Deb Ann left. I've heard with the government man, but no one's real certain. She sold the house herself, I guess, to a young couple, name of Vogrin. Nice folks—both blonde—people say. Both Catholic and none too talkative.

BLACKHAWKS

Let a few wear my off-game jersey during football season. *Let's go Hawks.* That's about it. I never took a girl on a date, though, not back at home in Stockton, when we were kids. After school, there was no place to go but her house or your car (and October to March was too cold for that last). We passed each other notes in class that said *After practice*; we fucked in the bus yard and under the stage, some days three at a time. No romance to it and too few of us not to be trading. *Your girl, your buddy's girl of two months ago, she had three of us trying to replace him. One afternoon he stood her up and she played with my boyfriend and me, to pass the time, waiting.*

Once a friend of mine got a gift card from his Chicago-aunt for Christmas. He lived out by Woodbine on the west end of town. Had to drive an hour to a theater that would take it. The girl that went with him, her name was Elizabeth, said it was two or three months to gelding season, the bull calves, good enough watching 'til then.

...A SINGLE CHARM IS DOUBTFUL: A DIPTYCH

A charm a single charm is doubtful. If the red is rose and there is a gate surrounding it, if inside is let in and there places change then certainly something is upright. It is earnest.
- Gertrude Stein, "Nothing Elegant"

When I think of Dorothy, I worry I've already forgotten her. Sight the least sense of my memory, she felt like an old woman, thin-skinned, and smelled of soda crackers. All I really have are aging words.

In her diaries, or what diaries were collected and kept by her youngest sister, Rita, my grandmother and the executor of her estate, Dorothy (Yohn) Smith logged daily, from the time she was thirty-five until at ninety-three dementia began finally to disrupt her memory or the habit, matters of secretarial importance—the places of her going, future appointments, books read, foods consumed, recipes tried and their relative quality as regarded by her tongue (as far as anyone knew she never cooked or baked anything, having only ever served houseguests cold cut sandwiches and raw baby carrots and always having brought the same Jell-O and pretzel dish to family gatherings and church potlucks alike, having once done so, goes my mother's version, for a Christmas party in the Seventies and, being thought so dear by all, the guests ate great plates of the stuff quickly thinking she'd feel loved and the mess would be gone forever), financial accounts labeled with cryptic abbreviations and written out (up to twenty-eight a day) as math problems, each done twice, in neatly parallel rows on legal pads and sheets of graphing paper stapled to their pages.

My first memory, the one that by date and detail I can to some degree verify, is of the farm auction, Dale then ten years gone and Dorothy worn down from dusting chaff and corn pollen from the entryway, washing mold from the limestone foundation, climbing three flights to the attic to assure herself no one had been there since she had last, checking same, staring out from a south-facing window at some fellow from Kussmaul, driving his pickup through her drainage, picking soybeans and tasting them, who she did not recognize because, though her husband had not been an especially clever farmer, Dale Smith had relished having done work he could call his own, so the Smith's eighty acres, since Dale had purchased them from his father in 1942, had been tended by his hands only, his and those of his family—his father, his brother, Dorothy's two brothers-in-law, and their seven sons, Dorothy and her sisters and their five daughters, whose work was not thought secondary, my grandfather would say, but so steady and constant that to speak of women's work, particularly the work of Yohn women, would be like speaking of a rain you were standing in. The Smiths had no children of their own.

Sales records show the auction lasted the whole of Labor Day weekend—house on Monday, equipment on Saturday, households and knickknacks after ten o'clock mass. Because Dale's grandparents had lived on the place before him and before and with them his great grandparents, all his father's side, because they, like Dale, had not been unfriendly, but like many of their generations had kept family in the home and been neighborly in the barns and yard, folks were curious. They came from both counties the property sat on to see what shape such a big house took on its insides, to pocket untagged forks and screwdrivers in their dresses and overalls, to speak ill or well of the sturdiness of furniture, whether or not it was for sale, to eat ice cream and pulled pork and stomp heels at a three-piece band Grandma says the auction house must have hired or had invited itself. To this day when I hear bluegrass, burnt sweet corn fills my nostrils.

People, including her people, assumed Dorothy bought her little ranch house in Lena with money from the sale of the farm. Knowing the Haas fellow who bought it to be, like her, a Lena State Bank man and not like himself, a First State Bank of Stockton one, Grandpa used to say they probably switched the ledger tickets from one desk to the next and charged everyone twice the interest for the trouble of the trade, an accusation he thought rye, I suspect, and one which dogged Grandma in years to come, the youngest of her sister LouAnna Mae's nine having become the president of the branch in the village of Warren, and so, though fifteen miles off, presumed involved in what most folks presumed nefarious. It may have been. But there's no evidence Dorothy ever did anything unseemly. No one she knew had money, and she did—which left us all a number of puzzles. And at the same time, in her ninety-four years, there wasn't a local murder gone unexplained, a cash register knocked over whose contents hadn't been accounted for, and if she had moonshined, nobody'd seen it, and if they had seen it, it would have been known: temperance never having gotten popular in the area, beer's been altogether too regular to fashion a man a time.

Her books may account for her assets. Grandma spent two years mapping patterns that never came to much, and by that time Dorothy's things had been distributed amongst her relatives or sold to her neighbors in a yard sale overrun with folks looking for evidence of her riches. They picked at the teeth of knives guessing if they were silver and sent children to the library for art books only to find Dorothy's paintings were common prints from artists a cheap motel would have cringed at hanging. And with the money gone and the taxes paid, the how of it got to be a useless thing, and no one much speaks of Dorothy.

That silence, for some of us, must indicate a poverty of our intentions, the inability to hold our minds to any subject longer than a television program might ask us, unless that subject is ourselves. And there has been a bit of that: the money having gone, per the will's allotment, evenly amongst Dorothy's fifteen nieces and nephews (twelve then surviving), those married have said those unmarried, and those unmarried have pronounced those divorced (the Yohn's being Catholic), which has led to the questions of those with four children as opposed to two, the legitimacy of tube tyings, the demands of charity to siblings and first cousins, though in driving distance rarely seen, the proper distribution of funds to the mentally incompetent and whether LouAnna Mae, sharp though she seems today, is getting too old to be managing large sums and what poor Marie in the state institution would do with the money anyway, stuck there and prattling on about her marriage to Prince Charles; and of course the common bickerings of who visited more and loved best—which is the closest any of us gets to telling stories about Aunt Dorothy.

Telling a story well and rarely, Grandpa used to say, is about all you can do to keep it from becoming a phrase, and a phrase is a tick off cliché, and, well, clichés never really were legends. Best to stick to accounts.

The dead are, after all, first the dead. So much so that reaching back to touch a chest, a neck, I feel a give before the body, and know that body so presently for this that if ever there were life in it, I wouldn't know it again by nature—the way it seems funny now to think of myself as a child playing with my grandfather's pocket change, pretending to the point of belief Lincoln and Washington might talk.

Dorothy died the winter after I turned sixteen, Devin fifteen. We were in the same class in school and divided by nearly a year. Both born in August, the fifth of '89 and the third of '90, I was registered to the class of 2008 by a mother who'd studied Winnicott and Jung in graduate school and he signed up for the same by a mother who was working the farm and machine tooling at the Dura plant and whose own parents, my mother's age, couldn't babysit much because they were both, at fifty-eight, still two-job working.

We were the only two boys in what was called "upper-level math," meaning our state test scores were above average and we were put in the classes of eight or nine girls who were also above average from the time we were ten-nine until the year Dorothy died.

That year our class of forty-five was invited to take course work at the Area Vocational Center, where students so inclined could train in the basics of auto mechanics, welding, pipe fitting, general skill sets toward becoming an LPN. Devin—even his family didn't call him Devin, only Fuzz and derivations—said he had low expectations of himself, meaning, I think, he knew his family couldn't put away for him or his two sisters to go to college but were also of a subset of rural pragmatists who preferred never to take loans— especially from the government—if loans could be avoided.

Fuzzy studied body work with some seriousness: used to drive around looking for dents on wheel wells and truck doors, offered to fix at cost what he thought he could get out. He sometimes took a loss on a paint job just to try something interesting he found on a farmer's field buggy—Those old Chevrolets, he said, with steel frames, bent in at strange angles. Shit you couldn't replicate.

I never took to automobiles, and while I liked playing football while I played it, never felt any propensity past practical exercise. I went to the weight room after school. I liked to stand above Fuzzy on the bench and watch veins creep over his knuckles while he finished. I liked to hear him tell me I was getting better, because, while he was younger than I was, he was more physical—a lean, buck-muscled boy with a Roman nose too high and large for his face and straight black hair that stood up and gave him his name, ears that leaned away from his head as if to act out a talent for listening.

After the weight room, we would cruise around country blocks in the Mercedes-Benz I'd taken as a hand-me-down from my older sister. The car was tank-like and had a loose stick shift. Fuzz would beg me to drive it, and every afternoon we played a game of thoughtful resistance before I handed him the keys. He would drive—sixty, seventy—too fast for gravel roads, and I would spout plot summaries of the novels I was reading, while Fuzz just sat there quietly, one hand over the wheel.

Aimless driving is a habit amongst teenagers in corn country, or it was from the time after the Second World War 'til the days even farm boys had their own cell phones. Fuzzy must have been one of the last of those driving boys. I, anyhow, was not. My mother bought me a phone early, liking the idea of being able to check in and hear that I was safe. We lived—we live—in a township north of the village of Stockton, seven miles south of Warren, on a farm my grandparents wouldn't, like Dorothy, sell but rented instead with the intent of passing that land to their children and from their children on to their grandchildren and on, into perpetuity, though my mother was the only one to have ever farmed the land herself, and since climbing the ladder from French teacher to school administrator hasn't had the time and so has joined the rest of the family, schooled in education, hydraulics, psychology, fine dining, human resources, art, interior design—I turned the damn thing off and told anyone who called we'd driven too far into the fields to get reception.

Fuzzy and I—I think I can speak for the both of us, though I shouldn't take for granted his silence—saw a little younger than we should have that the Land of Opportunity would distribute its resources to the two of us in different bundles. But, once the car was started, once we'd gotten south of the farmers who knew us well enough to wave us into a chat, if it was April or June and after a rain and he was driving and I'd shut up a while and he'd turned the radio on, I could watch the hills under a neon sky and pretend that wasn't true.

We weren't bored or reckless, really. Just doing something together. Truth told, that was a short time, and I still don't know that it had to be. Days felt long in our middle teens. There was time enough to daydream, and we did, though of things we'd do and never of solutions. Winter got on and Fuzzy started working at the Dairy Mart evenings. I would drive to Freeport and take gen eds at the community college. Sometimes when he was closing I'd call in an order under an alias and not pick it up so we could eat hamburgers when he got off, and I'd take him home. Eventually, the Dairy Mart bought a caller ID, Fuzzy saved up enough for a truck, he worked on cars and I read novels. We took to chasing women seriously.

We saw each other—in the halls, in pre-trigonometry. I'd embarrass myself to make him stay, would buy him dip, would beg favors, would challenge the Army recruiter who stood in the halls every few days at lunch time to a push up contest so that, when I lost, Fuzzy would come challenge and soundly beat him. At my peak, I could push up forty times, Fuzzy upwards of seventy. The recruiter, I think his name was Sgt. Daniels, claimed, fresh, he'd do a hundred straight. I never saw it, but worried truth in that.

Several months after Dorothy died, Grandma finally decided it was time to empty the ranch house and sell it. Had it been anyone else—Grandpa even—I think she'd have gotten right to the task at hand, as was with all things her habit. But Dorothy had been special to her, elder sister and friend. When they were younger, they and their husbands had shared farm chores, played euchre at night, put money in the same shoe box to send my aunt and mother and uncle all to college. Grandma took a long time to come around to the idea Dorothy could be gone. And when she finally decided to attend to the business of death and sorting, she simply walked up to me and told me to get a friend to help. If it'd get it done quick, she'd awful well pay him. So I called up Fuzz, and the two of us drove Grandma over to Lena, and while she went through the dishes and drawers, she asked us to bring everything up from the basement.

Fuzz was in a poor mood that day. Erika, the only girlfriend he ever kept for more than three or four weeks, had dumped him the night before, and that must have been one of the first times because he hadn't yet gotten stoic about it. Kept saying, "Give me your phone," and taking it and calling her to no answer and cussing while he handed it back and disappearing with an ottoman or nightstand up the stairs. A couple years later, after another split, he would join the Army and settle the argument by marrying her, so when he tripped an IED in Zhari Province meant for a truck, Erika became the beneficiary of his military life insurance and a pair of dogtags she later gave me. I've heard they buried him in a pair. Mine are pristine copy.

We didn't know any of that at the time. We were two boys differently unhinged. I'd say, "Let's get this couch up. It's heavy. I'm gettin' tired."

He'd lift his end and ask, "What's she payin' us?"

"How the hell should I know," I'd say. And we went on like that, ramming chair legs into walls and chipping varnish off the railings, until around four o'clock, Erika finally returned twenty or thirty calls to tell Fuzz he could go fuck himself.

"Bitch," he said, not to her but me. "I gotta go, man."

"Sucks," I said. We went up the stairs to tell Grandma it was time to leave, and she went downstairs and worried the damage we'd done and still asked if we couldn't stay.

We did, because there was nothing else to do once she'd asked, and because Fuzz didn't take enough pleasure in an argument to drive back to Stockton and have it out with Erika. We carried up the last few lamps and curtain rods. I vacuumed the floors, smelling of moth balls, all their shag in furniture patchworks of faded green, while Fuzz opened the one basement closet, large and packed inside with piles of file boxes so high he had to weave hand through box corners and the top of the jamb to even begin. He took ten or fifteen minutes getting out the first two or three boxes, and when he'd made the project easy access, if not all that reasonable, he gave up and said, "Fuck it."

"Fuck it," I said. I switched off the vacuum. Before it stopped whirring, Fuzzy had hauled back and kicked one of the boxes. Made a dent the rough shape of his shoefront. He sat down next to it then, complaining about a toe.

I said, "Man, don't do that shit."

He said, "Shit, there aint nothin' in here but your dead aunt's trash." He took a boxtop off and chucked it at me. It spun disc-like and turned near vertical before landing at my feet.

I said, "You are a weak Nancy pissass." I thought he'd hit me. I wanted to be hit. But he just sat there, one hand pressed to the carpet so hard his wrist bubbled out from the skin, throwing Dorothy's legal pads in my direction with the other, and the pads, pages splaying, each fell short.

"Fuck you," I said. "Fuck you."

"You are a bitch," he said. He'd emptied the box of legal pads but didn't want to touch me. He crawled over to another box, while I stood dumbly holding the neck of the vacuum, waiting for him to come. Stood, while he took from that box bankroll after bankroll of quarters, while he threw them at me and missed, every time, and the rolls sunk holes in the drywall and cracked open, drowning coins into the carpet.

You kissed me on the cheek and asked which great cluster of asterisks was Cassiopeia. I worried you'd think less of me when I told you I didn't know. Astronomy was never my strong suit. Likewise taxonomy, history, Greek classics.

It was one of those bright nights when the quarter moon could be seen, dimensional and peering out from a gray and cloudless sky. I apologized for not knowing and quoted you some bastardized line taken from Emerson or Whitman or Thoreau:

What would you do if the stars came out just once a millennium? And you told me the only answer that suited.

For the life of me, I can't tell you the names of the trees around us then, or of the shapes they made. Or of the sound of the wind rustling through them in that early autumn dream. Love, I have known it, but now it is gone, however vivid its memory.

I still drive down to the state park some nights and walk the paths we took, you with a steel canteen in hand and I with a knapsack full of wine and weed and prophylactics. We might have been high that night. I know we saved the water and emptied the bottles. It was all too romantic for making love. Just you and I, hand in hand on the path to that rock all the high school kids climbed. You were afraid we'd fall when I rambled up it to get closer to that three-dimensional moon. But you followed right behind me.

The road is paved now, and the first hundred yards of that path. A group of mothers asked the park board to do something about the rock, after some kid leapt off and smashed his leg up in the river. DNR's wrapped the base in barbed wire. Many of the trees have been hedged—Dutch elm disease—and the blacktop's made cutting through the park the easy way home for the Galena people leaving the highway taverns. Their red taillights strobe through the black between the trees.

I can't imagine in what light you see me, but the park itself is black, save for the flashlight by which I scratch my words to you. Even the sky holds just the tracking lines of Army jets heading north to Wisconsin. But from time to time, I stare upwards at the sky. When the stars come out, you said, "I would look at them."

SAMSARA AND OTHER LARGE ANIMALS

He died yesterday, at 93, my grandmother's friend, Merten Astor. Last I saw him was in the assisted living facility in Lena, his four-room apartment near the nursing clinic where Grandma used to work, where Grandpa last stayed, and then passed. This, seeing Merten, was a week before his birthday. He was planning festivities, invited me, and, though I'd promised I'd attend, I knew I'd be in St. Louis by then.

I assumed he'd forget.

"I'm going to have a ham," Merten said. He uncrossed his legs and crossed them again on the opposite side. "Doesn't that sound nice?" he asked with his chin in the palm of his hand.

Before Grandpa landed at the clinic, Grandma complained of his deafness—the rude things he said of people, loudly, within their earshot, the television tuned to volumes that rattled ear drums and throbbed temples. She leaned close to me to ask, "What did he say?"

"Ham," I said. "We'll be having ham at Merten's party."

"And pineapple," Merten said. "Dole. The rings."

"With pineapple. Ham with pineapple," I translated.

"Oh," Grandma said, "now that sounds nice."

How my grandparents came to befriend Merten Astor, I truly couldn't say. I asked Grandma once, to which she replied, "Oh, I don't have a clue. We've known him so long. How do you meet anybody?" As to Merten and me—whether we were friends or just acquaintances—I know we became familiar while I was a child. Though, Grandma's right, I don't remember when, precisely, or how. Like almost all of my childhood, it seems to me to have happened on one long and singular day. In memory, I am always grotesquely small, adults enormous, incomprehensible.

My grandfather took me out with his friend Gary Hofstadter, once, when I was seven or eight. We took the truck and picked him up at his house in town and drove the forty miles north to Monroe, Wisconsin. Ate at a place called Baumgartner Cheese Store and Tavern, where they must have had Swiss or Limburger sandwiches, thick with Dijon and raw onions, on thin-sliced rye. I would've had mine on white, the cheese, cheddar or Muenster or jack. I think the lights in the tavern were yellow, the paneling dark-stained oak. Above the bar, there was a pastoral mural—Fräuleins and cattle and verdant spring hills. A comic sign split its middle: LIMBURGER: DON'T EAT IT WITH YOUR NOSE.

I don't know what they talked about, none of it comes to mind. Like many moments in my childhood—and many still—my brain hasn't seemed to have stored the information it didn't understand. Which leaves me to wonder why I can, even now, envision that sign, because, it may be that I could read it at eight, but the joke must have been beyond me.

One answer, of course, is that the conversation, unlike the sign, was transient, moving. My grandfather, being a man of habits, probably shared Navy stories with Gary—they were both Pacific vets—and I'm sure I was captivated. It's just that Grandpa told those stories so often, I've logged them off in some other place where Gary's part has faded.

The truth is we probably visited Baumgartner's a dozen, two dozen, times. Perhaps more. What I mean when I speak of Grandpa's habits is that he never—in my recollection—did a thing once unless against his wishes and provoked by circumstance. He lived his life a mile, as the crow flies, from the house where he and his twin brother were born. His need to talk about The War, a second best to going again and running battleship engines and being young on the open sea.

Eggs and corned beef hash were his only breakfast, except once when my mother bought my grandparents a Hawaiian vacation—according to Grandma, he ate SPAM sandwiches there and complained the whole trip of the heat—and once in his middle-seventies, at the onset of dementia, when he refused to eat anything but canned red beets for two months straight. Then, whatever puree they fed him in the home.

We had to have visited Gary with some frequency. Because, though the time I am thinking of is the one I've come to imagine, after the trip to Baumgartner's in Grandpa's pickup, I remember looking for the little chair in Gary's curio.

He was a carpenter, Gary. He was tall and bald and knobby in a way I'd later associate with scientists and priests. He wore plaid—a lot—and made really interesting wooden furniture. I don't know where he sold it.

When I was in high school, Grandma bought one of his pieces, a full-sized pine bench branded with a whale, and set it in her entryway. Grandpa used to say to visitors, "You see that seat coming in? Made by a friend of mine. He give it to me. Give it to me, you believe that. They usually cost three, four hundred dollars." That was the only piece of Gary's I ever saw outside his home.

That day, after the cheese sandwiches, Gary not only invited us in—which was common courtesy—but he also asked Grandpa and me back into his shop. It was in his attached garage: there was an ancient planer in there and two band saws and a table saw that scared me because the blade looked like it was about to leap. The place smelled of oil and pinedust and of rich, dark lacquer and of the soothing carnauba wax still open on a bench. Two walls were lined with thick particle board counters, covered with tools of all kinds—hammers, drills, screwdrivers, woodturning chisels for his lathe, some I didn't recognize—and with parts of projects, failed or unfinished, lying prostrate like wooden animals wanting to be petted, and beside them the littlest chair I have ever seen.

I ran up to it, and Gary ran after me, a cautionary "Hey!" rising through the dusty air. The way I see it, up close, the chair was impossibly small, the size for someone who could sleep on my thumb. It was cherry and looked like it was made of toothpicks, a kitchen chair with dowels for its back. I stared at it, then up at the men, whose Navy caps brushed the ceiling. I stared at it and began to worry for it, so fragile. Gary said, "Careful. Don't touch it"—to me!—and Grandpa teased him, groaning, "Fee-Fi-Fo-Fum" and grasping at the air in the direction of the chair and putting his hand to his mouth as if he'd eaten it.

I screamed. And they both laughed, knobby Gary, and my enormous grandfather, looking a bit—I'd say now—like Chet Baker with some brawn. Gary picked it up, the chair, and set it in the palm of his hand. "How do you like that?" he asked Grandpa, who said, "How *do* you like that."

"Smallest chair I ever made. I've seen 'em, like this, go for three, four, hundred dollars. Hard to make 'em and not break the pieces. Most people've got to use glue, but I did it all mortise-and-tenon and dowling. Even got my little symbol on there, my whale spouting, see? I always get my whale on things, so people'll know it's mine."

It must have been just about then that Gary remembered me. He leaned over to show me the piece. Burned into the seat, a small whale, jovially smiling, a five-line spray spreading from its back. I reached over to pick it up, and he shouted, "No," like I was a dog, and took the thing in two fingers of the other hand so hard and quick, I thought he'd be the one to crush it. "It's fragile. So fragile." Behind him Grandpa was laughing.

Gary decided it was time to show us out then. He walked us back to the entryway, where he kept a coat rack and an ebony curio. He said, "It was good seeing you."

But Grandpa decided to get diplomatic. "Say, that's a fine chair you made," he pointed out. "You going to sell it? Don't know that I got four hundred dollars, but I do got a granddaughter whose birthday's coming up. She'd love a couple things like that for her dollhouse."

"Thank you, Merle," he said. "Awful kind, but you just don't get it." He said. "It's artwork. It aint dollhouse stuff."

Another version of this ends with Grandpa suggesting that the piece might be good for his friend Merten, "old mailman up in Apple River. Fellow collects dolls. Loaded too." And in this rendition, Gary doesn't think it's kind but says something nasty, like, "You think I'd sell my art to that SOB"—my grandpa and his friends would really swear like that, acronyms, always, in front of ladies and children—"so he can play around with it like a little girl?"

Either way or with a blending of the two, Gary produces a key from his pocket, and puts the little piece on the left side of the curio, in a place saved just for it.

We had to have come back: I remember looking for it. Remember being disappointed. And being disappointed despite the fact that I'd been back and knew it was missing. And being elated that it was back despite it having been missing. And being devastated because it was missing after having, like the young son of Jesus' tale, returned from its worrisome absence. And being made cynical by the whole experience but unflaggingly staring at that curio every time I came in... Those memories are more like feelings, ideas in my mind, but I have them. They are there. And so were we.

A Proustian cubist could paint me, in reality, this way: Andrew Abbar of two dozen moments, ages six to eleven, split and shifted so that the top of my head makes a totem of itself. I would be wearing the same four of five T-shirts, overlarge Grandpa-handmedowns, progressively more ragged as the image moves upward, and I would be looking with two realistically-shaped men at the blank space in the curio, where we three would be reflected in the glass, each of us twenty-four times.

Funny, it seems to me that I am, however unconsciously, bent on making compact narratives of my past. I used to do this. I used to do that. Moments stand out, and emotions, and objects of all kinds. Since Grandpa passed, I have periodically stopped at my grandparents' house to take from it things that remind me of him. Collected beside my bed now are a pair of scuffed leather cowboy boots and three caps that identify Grandpa as having been on the *USS Mississippi*, flaunting officer's insignia he didn't earn but later claimed right to, having been offered—the story went—a field commission if he agreed to stay on—which he didn't—after The War.

By the time I came to consciousness, that adult's linear sense of time, my grandfather had already become mentally unsteady. He was seventy-six when I was twelve. And it was about that time he began accusing Don Schwitz, the land tenant of his farms, of ripping him off—failing to tile the back forty, not putting nitrous on the soil, calling at strange times of night, creeping around the hallway outside my grandparents bedroom with a baseball bat in his hands.

Grandpa decided to kill him. He obsessed over it. My mother's told me he once drove me over to Don's house with a double-barreled twelve gauge. Luckily, it was Sunday, and the whole family was at church. I vaguely recall the way it looked when the Schwitz's front window shattered: a sudden asterisk appearing at its center, shimmering polygons dropping lackadaisically after into the gray living room and onto the fresh, dusty snow on the yard.

It was like that for years, the ones with my grandfather that are clearest to me. But I had and have a great affection for him. When he died, I spent weeks in a sorrow-drunk stupor, neither thinking of my loss nor able to focus on those things surrounding me. When I wake in the morning now and stare down at his boots, what comes to mind are the large and unreliable feet of his eighties. The brawny farmer who raised me comes mostly in still frames.

Most mornings I sit. I used to share my apartment with Jason, who moved to Arizona to chase peyote dreams and take crystalline pictures of the desert, to find, as he said, a new sound. Maybe I could have gone, but he didn't ask. So, I took up with Annie, who needed more order than I could give her, and gave me more orders than I could take. She lives in South City now and edits books for a Christian publisher. Her apartment is immaculate, as are her new boyfriend's clothes.

Me, I am trying to develop habits. To reduce dukkha in thirty-minute increments and accept the conditions of today. Annie's study, which was Jason's before, is empty, except for my pillow, an egg timer, a plastic California Raisin that reminds me of my mother, a statue of the Buddha, who sits behind me, not watching but sitting in silence as well. I wonder what he sees, if it is as the nameless drugs Jason used to buy us, that we took in summer, sitting at the river's edge and exulting in the shimmer of small ripples and of the shapes made by the abandoned grain houses where we saw out long days on endless journeys. Or perhaps, the Buddha's just half-asleep watching the glowing orange veins of his eyelids.

There is a story I read about him, and about a woman whose child had died. She heard that Gautama was specially blessed and came to ask for medicine, a cure for her dead son. But he wasn't Jesus crying for his friend—nor was she. Lost, Lazarus: what good would magic do? Lazarus died again, didn't he? And that's perhaps a damneder fate. Whatever is said, the Earth moves in plates, shifting mountains in its time. The Buddha instructed the woman to go to every house in town and collect a mustard seed from anyone who had never lost a loved one. She of course came back empty-handed.

I told my grandfather that story a month before he died. Sat at his bedside, holding his hand, talking to him like a child. It was a good day for Grandpa: he heard me, knew I was Andrew and not his son, John. "My dad used to tell me, it takes a big dog to weigh a ton," Grandpa said.

"Yeah?" I asked, hoping, as I so often have that the thing about to be said was of transcendent wisdom. Hoping that my grandfather would pass something infinitely meaningful on to me before leaving.

"It takes a bigger dog to shit a ton," he said laughing. "Makes sense to me." He laughed and laughed from deep in his chest, until his laughter turned a coughing fit and he vomited bile onto his bedsheets.

The unusual thing about Merten—the truly unusual thing—is that, though I hold those memories as in one day, I recall visiting his home, not in snippets but distinctly, not as once but dozens of times. I can parse them: I know specifically that I was seven and in the first term of second grade. I'd just gotten my midterm report card, and Grandpa had been telling everyone I'd gotten straight A's. Grandma had been wanting to visit, and for Grandpa the report card was a useful excuse. It's what we talked about. That and Merten's new toupee. He always wore toupees, combed in curvatures to his right side. By the time he died he had no less than five of them.

Merten's was no doll house. He was too cheap to buy vinyl siding or hire someone to repaint the worm-ridden wooden shingles that covered his garage and home. From the outside, his place seemed doomed to condemnation, unkempt, shabby, on the farthest edge of a dying township, that was itself surrounded by limestone cliffs, and so, pretty land but craggy, untenable for farming. The house stood beneath those cliffs, resting on an uneven lawn, odd cut with wadis from hard summer rains. The foundation, granite and cracked mortar, was exposed in surprising places. The garage, unattached, listed to one side and would, before my thirteenth birthday, collapse in a ragged pile of rotten and twice-used lumber.

Coming up to the screen porch, I ran my hand along the shingles to feel paint remnants scrape off against my fingertips. "Stop that," Grandma said. "What're you doing?" She took a swat at me with the back of her hand, though she was three feet out of range.

I was seven. I didn't stop because she seemed to quit paying attention. But a paint splinter got me almost immediately after. "Er," I cried.

"What is it?" Grandma asked. "Are you all right? Let me see it." She took my fingers and started picking at them.

"Serves you right," Grandpa laughed.

"Probably lead," Grandma told him.

Merten's porch had a hook-locked door. It hung loose, and when you knocked on it, it would bump into the jamb with a muffled thud. He never heard you knocking, not because his ears were especially poor but because the sound was so soft and the TV was turned up loud for Ferna. The problem with this was that Merten also hated intrusions. Even if he invited you, he wanted you not to step onto the porch without a formal, face-to-face welcome. So after Grandma knocked,

Grandpa and I had to walk around while we waited for Merten to see our shadows shifting across the living room curtains.

He came, eventually, as always, apologizing. "Oh, I didn't hear you. I must've fallen asleep."

"Hello, Merten," Grandma said, stepping back.

"Have you been waiting long?" Merten asked.

"What month is it?" Grandpa asked, and, "How you doing, Mert?" He walked right past my tiny grandmother to take hold of Merten's hand, sidestepping onto the porch.

"Oh," he said, morosely, "all right, you know. Well, come in, I guess. I'll tell you all about it."

As you entered Merten's house, you faced due north, towards the dining room and into the kitchen. Because, as Merten said, it seemed so pointless to own fine china and leave it dusting in the cabinets, his dinette set was always readied for himself, Ferna, and the six guests they could accommodate, each place complete with Depression glass and salad forks, chargers and embroidered napkins. We never ate there, except the one time, when the garage fell, and Grandpa and I drove over to pull Merten's things from beneath the rubble. Merten didn't help really, but stood around urging us to be careful of nails. At some point, he drove to the grocery store and bought Swiss cheese and sliced ham and mustard. After several hours of our digging around, he invited us inside for supper. He'd cut up the cheese and made sandwiches, which he set on paper plates, which protected the salad plates, which rested on the dinner plates on top of the chargers, all of which, save the paper, he washed while we finished the job, because despite his behests we be careful, we'd spilled crumbs on them all.

To the west were two beds, a dark oak and a fainting couch. No one ever used them. Merten's only relatives, his sister's two children, nephews both, lived in town. I can only assume he had an actual bedroom for himself; I never saw it. And Ferna, I was given to understand, slept in the wig room, or, when Merten was tired, was sometimes left in her chair. The living room beds were where Merten's dolls stayed. He had hundreds of them, all Victorian porcelain, pale as Merten himself, left as they were in the sepia yellow of his shuttered home. He spent most days on the east side of the living room, chatting with Ferna, who I never heard talk but who sat facing west towards him and the dolls so that she was always at an angle to the television while watching the soaps he said she adored.

Merten sat us down on his tweed couches. He told us about his youngest nephew, whose heart had been broke by a girl he thought would someday be the boy's bride. "Wasn't meant to be," Merten said, looking distractedly at the window shades.

"How are you?" Grandma asked, "Ferna?" A retired RN, and Catholic, she was convinced the catatonic are aware.

"That's too bad," Grandpa said. "You know, the boy there's doing real well at the school."

"That's nice," Merten said. "What did you get on your grades?"

"I—"

"I've bought a new hair piece," Merten said, finally settling into the chair beside Ferna. He was prone to turns and non sequiturs.

"All A's," Grandpa said. "Something happen to the old one?"

"Oh, no," Merten said. He patted his head, petted it, as if to keep stray strands in check. "This is the old one."

"Then why'd you buy a new one?" Grandpa asked, adding a bit more tactfully, "This one looks great."

"Merle," Grandma said. She whispered this curtly—she actually elbowed him in the ribs.

"Oh, it's okay," said Merten. "I just always wanted to be a redhead, you know. I always thought redheaded men were the most handsome. I dyed my hair once, right after I got out of the Army. But back then, you know, the dyes weren't very good, and it wasn't even, and it came out awful bright. It was really sort of carrot-colored."

"Oh, no," Grandma said, her face taking on a sharp rictus, as if she really were deeply worried about Merten's fifty-year-old snafu.

"It was so awful," he said. "I had to shave it all off and wear a hat until it grew back." He said, "I hate hats."

"I'm fond of 'em," Grandpa said. "Thank God." He pulled the *Mississippi* cap off his head and rubbed a palm across his scalp. Dandruff dusted his shoulders, and Grandma began picking at it, dropping it into a handkerchief she took from her pocket book.

"You're making a mess," she complained.

"Mine isn't growing back," Grandpa added, ignoring her. "Straight A's. I never got grades like that. Barely graduated."

Merten unfolded his legs and came to his feet. "That's good," he said, in the same soft and measured voice he always had any time he wasn't irritated. "Your grandpa's proud of you," he added. "Anyway, my wig? Would you like to see it?"

"I'd love to," Grandma said.

"Would you like to see it?" I think Grandpa was putting his cap back on, but I'd taken to looking at Ferna, whose lip, I'd just noticed for the first time, was swollen an unnatural purple on one side and sagging under the weight of itself. "Andrew?" Merten asked, "Would you?"

This morning, I woke up early and drove the five hours north to home. Mom greeted me at the door, said, "How you doing, hon?" I told her fine, and she asked if I minded watching Grandma for the afternoon. Mom had plans, and Grandma'd been a pain. "Doc says she's got a UTI. He got her started on antibiotics a couple days back, but she's still loopy."

"Yup," I said.

"You know, moody," Mom said. "She'll get pissed because I've washed the dishes and forgot her fork on the table. Then she'll walk off and fall asleep in her chair."

"Shit," I said.

"Yeah," she said. "I just need a day off before the funeral. She's been all wound up."

Grandma was in the bathroom, so the TV was muted, an elderly woman yelling silently to Life Alert for assistance that would certainly come. "Let me show you this," said Mom. "Your Uncle John sent it to me for my birthday."

On the table, three California raisins, with rubber faces vaguely reminiscent of famed jazz men and Motown players, standing on a brown plastic stage. Mom went to it, bent over, pressed a button in front of Little Richard cum dried grape. *Here I am, Bay-be. Signed, sealed, delivered…* Behind Little Richard, a guitarist, left, a saxophonist, right—from my perspective. Their six plastic legs leaned one way, click, under the music—*I'm yours!*—leaned the other way, click. *Signed, sealed…*

My grandfather used to sing the "Notre Dame Fight Song," not because he was a Fighting Irishman—his only college was a partial year of officer candidate's school at Oberlin, while he waited for transfer to the Pacific. Grandpa just liked bad jokes. His version stuck to the tune but replaced cheer with beer: *Beer! Beer for ol' Notre Dame. You bring the whiskey; I'll bring the same. Send some freshmen out for gin, and don't let a sober sophomore in. We never stagger, we never fall. We sober up on wood alcohol. While the loy-al fac-ul-ty lay drunk on the ballroom floor.*

It may be that I've forgotten something, but it seems to me that this was one of three songs he ever sang, along with "It Ain't Gonna Rain No More, No More" and a certain half-melodious drone he made during family rounds of "Happy Birthday."

The music might be a mnemonic device. I had a high school teacher who asked her classes to learn the quadratic equation to the tune of "Jingle Bells"—or was it "Joy to the World?" Either way: Negative b plus or minus square root of b squared minus 4ac, all over 2a. I can't tell you what you'd use it for. There was no purpose to the melody. And when I think about this, I think sometimes that all things must come like music, melodic lines, at once memorable and ephemeral, shifting and undulating at every repetition—the articulation different, the speakers in the stereo worn a little more each playing.

This afternoon, Grandma and I drove up to Baumgartner's for an outing. The house seemed too bound, everyone gone but us and the dog, Maggie, and grandma senilely repeating to me that it was too bad about Merten. He was old and unwell, she kept saying, but he was still pretty with it. And Grandma has so few friends left.

Baumgartner's hasn't changed much since I was a kid. Still the same two rooms, cheese sales and tavern. Same Swedish-German décor. Same comic T-shirts sold upfront. A cow bell made for Bunyan's Babe hangs above the cash register (Ring for Service). The mustard horseradish, though—don't say Dijon, which is French, and different. The mural, not Fräuleins, not even one mural but two, one for each room: above the cheese counter a darkly shaded country scene, devoid of animal life. Above the liquor bottles, humanoid beer steins charging likewise humanoid bottles of wine, who've come to all fours to uncork themselves as cannons. In the sky between them, an inscription the bartender roughly translated as, *When Beer and Wine go to War, who will be Victor, who will be Vanquished.* "Weirdly phrased," he said, "so it'll rhyme."

"Strange," Grandma told me while I sat her down in a booth and ordered us Swiss cheese and limburger sandwiches.

What is most remarkable to me is not the strangeness of this place nor is it the restaurant's stasis over time, rather my ability to forget things so wildly strange and static. To misremember places I have come to hold so dear to my history. Limburger is pungent, more so than the cellophane cheese eater I've become recalled. The sign warning me about this is reasonably small, almost unnoticeable, and sitting to one side of the bar.

"It's too bad about Merten," Grandma told me.

For the child, divided in his attentions by the myriad newness of things, it is perhaps only the redundant that can remain at all intact. The year I graduated college I moved to the Illinois side of St. Louis, where I lived cheaply as a substitute teacher, driving to the city in the evenings to play jazz standards on street corners and in the blues bands that would have me. Some nights, I would stay, sleep in Jason's bed, spread eagle, staring at the ceiling to maintain the feeling that the apartment might fly us away, and when the mornings came, always too soon, I would often wander aimless while Jason lugged off to work at the university. Most days, though, I managed to answer the six a.m. phone calls, hunting someone to teach.

More often than not, it was the upper grades—high school band in Collinsville, English or civics in East St. Louis. But, on occasion, when the weather was poor, or on a Friday before a three-day weekend, or when a class was especially rambunctious and some managing secretary thought a male presence would quell them, I might find myself in a preschool or kindergarten classroom, attending scraped knees and flipping cards.

The days I taught elementary probably number in the single digits, but from my first hour in a room full of six-year-olds, it was evident to me their need for order: popsicle sticks in the calendar pockets must happen before students choose between lunch pizzas, pepperoni or cheese; math worksheets may be done on the floor, though handwriting sheets cannot; the teacher must stop everything when given a hug. Any divergence from these patterns will result in twenty-five tiny, shrieking voices calling, *Mr. A! Mr. A!*, a single tattler on your pant leg, and mass, dog-piling hugs to temper a mood-shifting substitute.

So there I was, a sunburnt child in the dim, mothball-scented living room of a seventy-five-year old man, who had reappeared from Ferna's closet wearing a redhead's toupee. He was almost luminescent, in the way that Fifties film posters are, painted in shades meant to look bright but seeming flat somehow, barn paint on a tin plate: his shirts were pale colors, that afternoon off-white, tinged with an egg-yolk yellow, dull paisley amoebas crawling all around it; his pants, the same pants, or the same make and model of pants he always wore, dark-brown highwater slacks that exposed argyle socks and the tops of his oxblood shoes. Merten's glasses came directly, I am certain, from the yearbook photo of a female Baby Boomer who would forever regret her childhood taste, specs white and wing-tipped, frames thicker than my thumb.

"You look so handsome," my grandmother told him.

Grandpa was busy making faces at Ferna, sticking his tongue out and raising his eyebrows, trying to get her to do the same. She blinked twice, rapidly, and Grandpa clapped his hands with childlike excitement. He looked quickly to me and smiled as if we understood each other. "They're going to take you for a mick, Mert."

"Merle," Grandma said, "that's mean," shifting her body to him, her back to me. "That's a sin. We're Catholic."

"I'm Flemish," Merten explained. "My people."

"Is that in Ireland?" Grandma asked, turning to face Merten.

"Deutschland," Grandpa said, still excited, standing up just for the movement of it.

Merten frowned. Dropped the thought. Let his face soften. Adjusted his wig. "Belgium," he said to Grandma. "My people are Dutch."

"Well, isn't that something?" said Grandma, and to no one, "Isn't it."

I stuck my tongue out at Ferna. She didn't do anything that I could see, but Grandma cursed Grandpa under her breath and backhanded me on the shoulder closest her. I slid into my chair, out of reach, then wriggled my eyebrows. Nothing doing.

"There are lots of redheads in Belgium," Merten told us. "I met some during the War."

For a while we all blinked, quickly, slowly. Grandpa sat down.

Merten sat down. "Lots of beautiful redheads in Belgium."

"Nothing but black hair in Japan," Grandpa said. "No surprises there. A few of them dyed it blonde. But those were all," he decided on, "women."

"Oh," Merten said. He wrapped his fingers around the claws of his chair. "I see."

Grandma blinked. She looked flatly at me.

"I've got something to show you," Merten said.

The day I turned eighteen, a video arrived, from the wife of Grandma's dead twin brother. Gretchen, her name, had had her eldest son convert her 16mms to DVD, and thought we might enjoy them. Grandma and Grandpa were living with us then. She couldn't take care of him, or bring herself yet to put him in the home. We, my grandparents and mother and I, spent most of that morning watching silent images of my relatives as children and young parents, having picnics in the farmyard, playing wiffle ball and games of tag.

Grandpa didn't have much to say about them. He sat in his chair smiling glibly and scratching at dandruff. "There's some pictures of our wedding," Grandma offered. "I wish we had film of that."

"Yeah," Mom said, "that would be nice."

"That would be nice," said Grandma. "And Niagara Falls. He never took me anywhere. That was something special. Real pretty. That drive. The falls."

"Heck of a trip," Grandpa said.

"Took me to Ohio, where he went to college," Grandma explained. "We had dinner with an old girlfriend of his."

"Oh?" Mom asked.

"Oh, she was married then," Grandma said, as if to assure us. "To a big fellow. Kind of dumpy. We had supper at their house. Right there in the middle of it, she turns to me and says, 'I hate you.'"

"What?" I laughed. In the background, the movie was still running. Grandpa was wrestling, there, with my uncle John. A German Shepherd was leaping on the pile.

"Said I ruined her life. Was sure Merle was the only man could've made her happy."

"She was already married," Mom logicked.

"Yeah," Grandma said, lamentably. "We were supposed to stay with them, but I told your dad we were going ahead and getting a motel. I won that one." Uncle John started crying. Grandma rushed onto the scene to hug him. The dog put his front paws on Grandma's back. Grandpa started laughing.

He said, "I don't remember that."

⁂

Merten took my hand, not as adults normally did, limp and clammy, staring ahead with absent minds. A tall man, six-two or six-three, he hunched over to lock fingers with me, waiting patiently as I hopped out of my chair, and walking me to the opposite side of the room.

My grandparents, not invited, stayed on the couch, watching, I assume, as Merten led me center stage, to the rug between the beds where his dolls spectated my confusion. He let go.

"Stay here," Merten said delicately. "This is very precious."

On the west wall was a laundry chute, a door to a basement I'd never seen. But in that moment, he opened that door to me. The shaft had been covered with particle board, on which sat a chair I could've hid in my hand. And on that chair was a doll, the smallest, dressed in velveteen green, her orange hair braided halfway down her back. I could see it, completely. From where I was standing, could see everything from her pin black eyes to the strings that tied her legs to the torso beneath her skirt. For a time that seemed endless, I watched that doll, unchanging but aging, as Jonah, Leviathan constrained. In that final room of her still life, the doll, pale as formaldehyde will make us, was unreachable. I lifted a hand up to her. Behind me they were all watching.

And Merten said, "I know."

ACKNOWLEDGMENTS

> To Liv to Love
> To Live for Love;
>
> For Ever.

Having spent much of my adult life working in and around writers and the publishing industry, I've long believed that books should not come with acknowledgments pages but with credit reels, and perhaps at the beginning, before reader opinions have been formed about "the author." The author is often at fault for a book's flaws, but never solitary in creating its virtues.

This is crucial. I didn't write *More Hell*, I directed the writing of *More Hell* with the constant aid and support of beloveds who read, edited, researched, financially backed, emotionally crutched, brought sense to, occasionally (re)phrased, and permitted me to manipulate their lives' stories for my eccentric vision of truth through fiction.

When I miss a number of names and explanations here in my thank yous, it's not because my publisher held me to page limits or because I intentionally ignored generosities; it's because this project took a long, long time. I've been blessed throughout that era by the kindnesses of others, so much so that I've been able to forget more than a few for their abundance. This is the definition of good luck.

So let's start here…

A great deal of this work took shape because my friends, (now Dr.) Zachary Lawrence and Chris Duncan, challenged me to get a version of the following anecdote under academic eyes:

> Two teenaged boys are stoned. One sits at the desk in his bedroom with one hand down his jeans, one fist pounding the desktop. He is weeping. His friend asks what's wrong, and he announces that he has "ball cancer. I'm gonna die."
>
> Having been buddies since they were small, they blubber together—sniffling, "I love you, man;" "I love *you*, man;" "I'm going to miss you, man."
>
> This existential crisis/love fest ends when the boy with ball cancer announces, "Dude, it's been there the whole time. It's just that string, that lumpy string that holds your ball on," and the two teens sit in the aftermath and present of their mortality.

A longer, hopefully more nuanced version, of this tale once appeared in the titular performance piece "More Hell," and, though that story was cut to refine the final collection, I'd like for this origin to be known.

Little in my literary life would have been possible in the past half-decade without the friendship, mentorship, and support of Andrew Nash Gifford. My work with him at SFWP has been nothing less than a godsend; outside this book and my scattered writings, my life at SFWP has been my professional oeuvre.

Many other writers, artists and companions—including those I've served as editor for—have contributed to this book. Chief among them, but in no particular order, are Monica Prince (the world's tallest and most beloved choreopoet), Manuel Muñoz, Farid Matuk, Paco Cantu, Brandon Wampfler, Valerie Vogrin (literary mother), Aaron White, Sharonne Meyerson, Allison Funk, Megan Hudgins, Chris Cahill, Eileen Joy, Geoff Schmidt, Jason Braun (Beast and brother in the pen as arms), Alison Hawthorne Deming, Fenton Johnson, Dave Pedersen (Rockford's own Virgil), Jon Riccio, Matthew "The Docktor" Schmidt, Ingrid Claire Wenzler (spiritual Patti Smith and Hemingway), Jon Miller, Bree Sheaffer, Kate Bernheimer, Jae Towle Vieira, Natalie Griner, Lauren Greve, Jay Bungay, Nick Greer, Nikki Whitaker Malley and her era of the KJE, especially Jake Dylan Hawrylak, Kevin Malley, and Josh Garties.

I owe a debt to several colleagues and employers for letting me, knowingly or not, steal time from practical and capitalist matters to write on the clock, including Lucie Teichman and Inwork Inc., Trade Union's Ayo Balogun, my friends and Iowa City colleagues Sarah Kunch, Dani Worrel and Yimmy Corpus, Julie Cecchini at RIT, Charles Jensen at the UCLA Extension, and Gerard Ramos, Ricardo Ramos and Sam Peake at ROL Campgrounds.

While my education hasn't often aided my art, having attended Stockton High School, Highland Community College, Knox College, American University, Southern Illinois University Edwardsville, and the University of Arizona gave me the pleasure of working with the likes of Lydia Breunig, Robin Metz (mentor and great spirit), Barbara Tannert-Smith, Heather Heckel, Michael Stoops (of the National Coalition for the Homeless), John Don Hamman, as well as my favorite uncles, Casey Sims Kenna and Ron Pfeifer, to whom I owe more credit for this book than anyone.

The editors and volunteers at the non-profit 1-Week Critique keep my faith in literature alive, as do the kids at the Iowa City Public Library who attend our workshops. A dear thanks to Caleb"Spud" Schmidt, Caty Cox, Patience Wiley, and the one and only Victoria Fernandez for keeping the coals alive into the future.

Jo Daviess County, particularly Stockton and Galena, Illinois, and Monroe, Wisconsin appear heavily as settings in this book. Several early blurbers helped contextualize what this meant, including Steve Conn and Dennis Gage. I couldn't be more grateful for the attention they gave this work. The Anamosa Public Library was incredibly patient with my occasional appearances in their stacks to ask obscurantist questions about the Driftless Area.

I am and keep on by the love of my family—Karen Sirgany (Ma!), my grandparents Rita and Merle Baylor, Dorothy Smith, Mattie Gulyash, Lauren Smith (my ride or die), Maggie, Teddy, Ellie, Hera, HW, and the Widge!

My massive, undying love and gratitude to the team at Whisk(e)y Tit: friend, editor and writer of immense gifts K. Hank Jost, patient and wondrous cover artist

Sébastien Derenoncourt, and literary wet nurse and auntie in the mission to keep indie lit alive, the one and only Miette Gillette, who amidst her stacks of loud and daring pages, found my ode to Gina Berriault, and decided to publish something odd and quiet.

Finally, thank you, reader. If you've come to this page, you've presumably picked that something up and given this book a little of your life. As says my friend Jerry Wayne Longmire, "The greatest gift you can give to someone is time."

This book shares its dedications with Christopher "Papa" Thornton, in payment of a bet.

Volo ut sis.

Adam al-Sirgany

ABOUT THE AUTHOR

Adam al-Sirgany is an Arab-American editor, essayist, poet, short story writer, busker, and nomad born and raised in the Driftless Midwest; he's been drifting ever since. Adam works as the Acquisitions & Developmental Editor for the independent press SFWP, teaches for the UCLA Extension Certificate Program in Writing, Editing, and Publishing, and is the Executive Director of the literary education non-profit 1-Week Critique. When he isn't being literary, he manages campgrounds for ROL Destinations and hangs out with his family, Ellie Cat, and Hera the Dog. More about Adam can be found on his website: adamalsirgany.com.

ABOUT THE PUBLISHER

Whisk(e)y Tit is committed to restoring degradation and degeneracy to the literary arts. We work with authors who are unwilling to sacrifice intellectual rigor, unrelenting playfulness, and visual beauty in our literary pursuits, often leading to texts that would otherwise be abandoned in today's largely homogenized literary landscape. In a world governed by idiocy, our commitment to these principles is an act of civil service and civil disobedience alike.

9 781952 600623